Poppy Seeds on a Grave

A COLLECTION OF SHORT STORIES

MIRKO MARKOVIC

Poppy Seeds on a Grave

Illustrations by Luka Hobbs

tellwell

Tellwell Talent
www.tellwell.ca

ISBN
978-0-2288-4577-5 (Paperback)

Table of Contents

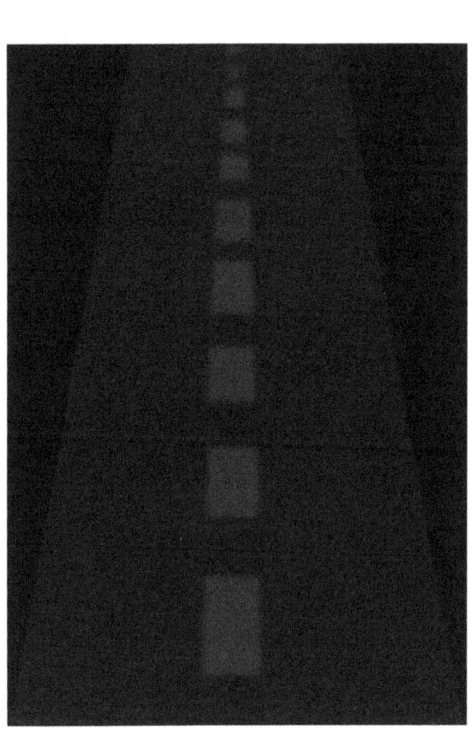

A Letter from Matthew

When I was six years old, I was diagnosed with a chronic respiratory disease which necessitated that I permanently remain in a ventilated, negative pressure room or wear a respirator if people came in to visit me. As a result, my family always made sure that anything I needed was in my room, which became my entire world. I was the only tween who wasn't out on the streets for Halloween, playing in the snow all winter or causing chaos on summer nights. My mother told me that I was God's special guy and that he was keeping me protected in here from the evils of the world. It didn't take long for me to become resentful of anyone or anything that related to a god who would condemn me to this fate. Today, I still hate him and everything he created. I don't resent my mother for telling me what she did—maybe she didn't even believe it. There's a good possibility that she only said it to give me a sense of a life while being entombed in my room.

Thankfully, I grew up at a time when the Internet was so widespread across the world that I was ensured some contact through it. My friends were all virtual, and they were spread across the planet. I don't think I had a single friend who actually lived in my neighbourhood, or even my city. In fact, I think I became something of an urban legend to the other children. They knew I existed and lived permanently in the house. Fuck, they even knew which window was mine. The number of times someone reached out in a meaningful attempt at contact paled in comparison to the times that eggs or other less hygienic things, like dog shit or water balloons filled with urine, were thrown at the window. I would spend countless hours sitting in front of my window overlooking the neighbourhood street, watching the world pass by. It was my private movie and I always made sure to sit just far enough in the dark of the room that my presence wouldn't garner any unwanted attention.

By the time I was thirteen I began to notice the brown-haired girl who lived across the road three houses down from me. I never knew her real name, but I called her Nicole. She spent a lot of time outside, often with other girls from the neighbourhood. One August afternoon that I spent watching her comes to mind. That day her hair was down, and the light from the sun brought out the natural highlights. As she walked from her front deck to the yard to talk to people and back, her hair shone with accents of red. She was wearing a white T-shirt with pink writing on it, light blue shorts and white sneakers. Early in the afternoon, a few of her friends came to the house and sat on the front-porch step, reading magazines and thumbing through their cell phones. They then left for a while to go to the park, mall or any number of other places free and pretty girls went on summer afternoons. Nicole came back alone and walked in her front door, and I waited patiently for the sun to set. As darkness fell, I returned to the artificial light of my computer screen, knowing I wouldn't see her again until the next morning. I spent countless days watching her and wondering if she even knew I existed. I loved the girl I believed she was, but I know I was nothing more than a dark window down the street to her.

With the coming of every September, I would watch as the other kids left to go to school. I stayed where I was, as I was. I was lucky enough to be able to do school from home, so at least I felt I had something in common with everyone else. I could only assume everyone else was as happy as I was to get back to school. The studying didn't get me overly excited, but I knew that with the coming of school I had more reason and opportunity to be in contact with people. It was impressive how many other kids around the world were learning online like I was. We were all happy to have the opportunity to talk with one another and be somewhat on the same page as other kids around us.

During Grade 6, I met one of my good friends, Amir. He was doing school online because his father travelled a lot for work and had to take his family from city to city and country to country. It all sounded pretty impressive to me, and I was envious of his changing scenery, but he resented his lack of roots. I could understand where he was coming from, but I would have loved to have been able to have half the change in life that he did. Amir and I played a lot of games online with each other. He didn't really enjoy role-playing games, preferring instead to play classic board games like chess. I wasn't as involved in them as he was, but after a few months of playing chess against Amir I started becoming a pretty accomplished player. I always had my hands full playing against him, but when I got to the point that I would win two out of every five or six games I knew I was making some real progress. The fact that Amir was constantly moving from one place to another probably gave him the sense that he was watching the world around him in the same way I was: unable to form meaningful in-person friendships.

My relationship with my family was always great. Like everyone else, we had our moments that were probably exacerbated by the fact that everyone had to take care of me, and I always felt like a burden on them. Otherwise, we were tight. My brother Francis spent a lot of time with me, and I know he didn't have to. He was two years older and had every reason and opportunity to go out with his friends or girlfriends. I always wanted to ask him the name of the brown-haired girl, but I worried that knowing who she was would make it harder for me. Today I regret not knowing. Francis never complained about having to spend time with me. It never appeared that he felt like he was filling time when he would suit up and come in my room to hang out. We always called it "suiting up" when he came to see me. He had to put on a mask to make sure that he didn't transfer any airborne bacteria that could make me sick or kill me, and a gown and other protective gear. We figured "suiting up" sounded less medical. I'm not sure if anyone else would agree, but Francis and I did and it worked for us. He would refuse to watch movies with his friends and wait till he could get them on DVD or download torrents so he could watch them with me. The best day was when he and one of his friends, James, brought up my dad's 60" LED TV so I could get a better movie-viewing experience. My dad cried when he saw us that night.

My parents gave up everything for me. I was never made to feel like I was an outcast in the family or a burden on them. They did everything they could to make sure I stayed a part of the family after I couldn't spend as much time with them. I know my mother had a really hard time when I stopped being able to have family dinners with everyone. To make her feel better, my dad wired up a webcam in my room with half of a dining room table that he refinished to look like our table downstairs. On the other end was a webcam and screen so we could all see one another. A lot in our house was rewired and renovated so that I could have access to food and drinks, and so that I could have as normal a life with my family as was possible. I know Francis and my dad hated that I couldn't go hunting or fishing with them, but I never had any negative feelings about it. It wasn't anyone's fault. It was what it was.

Sometime in the autumn of 2013, things started to change. I was watching the news and they reported that a man had died in a hospital in New Zealand of some type of bacteria that was resistant to every known type of antibiotic. Whatever he had contracted while on vacation in Asia was immune to everything doctors could throw at it. The original story didn't receive much attention on TV, almost like it was a passing story that didn't matter. At the time there was too much going on. The US was at war in Afghanistan and Iraq, Syria was imploding, and crazy North Korea was, well, being crazy, so it was a story that didn't matter. Plus, it was only one case. It was probably about a year later when the next few cases started hitting the news.

People were dying from this illness, which was still completely resistant to everything available. What made things worse was that nothing that was developed could fight it. Whatever this bacteria was, it had mutated to be resistant to everything. Short of fire, I suppose.

The first few cases that hit us made big headlines. Most people didn't react to it because we had survived SARS, bird flu, pig flu, chicken flu, mad cow and every other type of animal illness that there was. But this was different. This wasn't something that had mutated from an animal strain to a human strain. It didn't take long for the cases to pile up. First, it was people who had travelled from infected places in the world, and from there healthcare workers and police started getting sick. Then the panic started. I mean, when the people who are supposed to make you better start dying and the people who protect you start dropping, there's nothing to stop the evil people from taking advantage of things. But it wasn't just the bad guys, it was also the scared people. Nobody knew what to do.

My family started squirrelling away supplies in the house, lots of dried or canned food and water. It wasn't long before my dad renovated the spare room to be attached to my room so that I could get to supplies myself. I didn't really understand it at first. I was only fourteen, going on fifteen. A couple months later my dad got sick. It didn't take long; the bacteria works really fast. That's not to say it wasn't painful. I could hear him the first few nights reeling in pain downstairs in the den. It was made into a makeshift infirmary because the hospital wasn't taking any more patients. The risk to people not infected was too high and they were trying to mitigate the spread of the virus in the hospitals. Officially people were told to stay home, avoid contact with anyone and to treat it like a serious flu, and once a treatment was available they would start distributing it. In reality, people were just sent away to die. Two weeks is what it took, and Dad was dead. I don't know what they did with his body, but I know that funerals were being banned for anyone who died of the illness; instead, cremation was mandated. I'm pretty sure that funeral homes were becoming akin to the fires of hell, considering they were burning so many people in those years.

After my dad died, my mother kept spirits up and continued to stock supplies for her and Francis and me. But I think her spirit broke the day Francis got sick. I knew something was wrong when he didn't come to watch the news with me for two days. The next time I talked to him it was over webcam and he looked like a ghost. His skin was white as a piece of paper. His voice was weak and laboured and he could barely keep his eyes open or hold the tablet to steady the webcam. He told me that I had to keep going, and that everything would be okay. We joked a bit about how the illness was being reported on the news, but every time he laughed I could see that he was in pain, so over the next couple days I stopped making jokes because I couldn't stand to see him in agony. Seeing Francis get sick and then knowing that he died was almost too much for me. He had always been there for me. Everything that made me feel like I was a part of the world around me was because he wouldn't let me not be a part of it, and now he was gone.

Mom never recovered from losing Francis and Dad in such a short time. Our conversations became shorter and less frequent. Her voice was always empty, and every effort she made from that day on was to make sure I had enough to keep me going until a cure or treatment could be found. For the next couple months there were contractors in our house that Mom knew, setting up heating and power for my room that was not dependent on the city's power grid. Her emptiness got worse over time, and I couldn't help but feel guilty for everything. I knew she was doing this just for me, and I also knew that we didn't have the money to pay for these renovations. She sold a lot of our stuff, but to make sure that all the work was done she had to find other ways to pay for it. Between losing Francis and now losing herself to make sure that I could live, she wasn't Mom anymore, and I still can't forgive myself for this. She became the pariah of the neighbourhood. Friends stopped coming to see her, and it wasn't just the sick ones. Neighbours didn't look at her when she was outside cleaning the yard of leaves or snow.

Through all this, she lost everything. When she finally fell ill there was nobody who could take care of her and there was nothing that I could do. We talked over the webcam and she explained to me what was going to happen. It was the most surreal conversation I've had in my life. She basically explained to me that she was going to transfer all the supplies left for her into my supply room, and then the power and heat would be set to go until it was cut, and I would be on my own until a cure or treatment could be found. She assured me that there would be one, but it wasn't going to happen fast enough for her to benefit from it. I had to listen as she told me that this was going to be our last conversation and that she was going to leave. She didn't know where she was going, and she could barely look at me during the conversation. The exhaustion behind her eyes left me with an empty feeling that permeated through every bone and muscle. Whatever ounce of fight that had once existed in her had been drained, and I knew I was truly alone—in fact, it was now clear I had been alone for some time now. The next morning, I sat at my bedroom window and watched as my mother trudged down the street and out of sight. The last memory I have of her is watching as she disappeared, coughing in obvious pain.

The three people closest to me were gone. All I had left was to watch the world around me and talk to Amir. He and I kept in contact, but as time marched forward our chess games became less and less frequent. He explained that his father had decided the best course of action was to keep moving and hope to find somewhere the illness hadn't taken over completely.

Eventually, our conversations stopped. Six hundred and fifty-two days have passed since we last talked, and the only reason I know this is because it is recorded as the last conversation from our chats. I wonder if Amir's family was right to keep moving. I know that our family stayed put because of me, and that didn't help us. Everyone here died, and everyone in our neighbourhood who stayed eventually got sick too. Maybe Amir is still moving and just can't get an Internet connection where he is. Whether or not that's the case, I've given up on the hope of playing chess with my friend again.

I spent every morning watching the brown-haired girl's house, holding my breath, hoping to see her come outside. She did, every morning, some days for longer than others, but it wasn't long before she was gone too. I don't know what ended up happening to her, but one day she and her mother got into their car with luggage and what I can only surmise were a few coolers of supplies, and, like my mother, left down the street and out of my sight. I hope that she is okay and that wherever she went the illness didn't penetrate, or some kind of a cure was found. I can only imagine what happened to her.

I don't know who I am writing this for. I can only imagine that if there is anyone left anywhere that they won't be around here. It has been a few years since the illness spread across the world, and any talk about finding a treatment for it stopped a long time ago. Talking about a treatment would be like talking about the productivity and profit margins of Santa's workshop. It's nothing more than a fantasy, and pinning one's hopes on it is fruitless. I have sat here at my window and watched as the world slowed to a grinding halt. The road has started to crumble and the grass on the yards has started taking over the sidewalks and pavement. I can't help but feel that I was the illness, because surely the only thing that remains is that bacteria, the illness it carries, and me. I've tried to be vigilant and continue, if for no other reason than my mother. But it has been too long since I've seen anyone or talked to another person. I simply can't continue. I've watched from my window as everything around has disappeared.

I've printed this letter in the hope that someone finds it. If you are reading this, look to your right. Behind that door is the room where my supplies are. There is more than enough dried and canned food and water to keep you going for years. It would have been enough to keep me going if I could have continued. The door in front of you is my room, so please go to the right, because there is no reason for you to see what is in here now.

To whoever is reading this letter, please don't forget my story.

Sincerely,
Matthew

How You Have Eluded Me

I have to admit that typically, when something is more difficult, it is proportionally more rewarding. The amount of work I have put into you would have led even me to believe that this would be a more celebratory day. Take that as a lesson you can carry with you for all of eternity. I have been at my work for far longer than you've had the opportunity to frustrate it. So your luck and evasion were of little frustration for me. Although, I do have to admit I thought I would have gotten to you much sooner than I did. Regardless, here we are now. It really is unfortunate that we have to be talking like this tonight. I pictured it a bit different. I thought at the least I could visit your house, see your family and all the pleasantries awarded to any of your regular guests. You always were the most gracious of hosts, everyone else told me this. Ned, Mike, Dave—they all said it.

But rather than visit you at home, I'm here to see you. Really I'm no different than anyone else you've had come visit you recently. I will concede that most of them—okay, probably all of them—were really hoping for you to recover; whereas I . . . well, I was confident that this was the end of the line for you. You're probably wondering what I mean by "something is more difficult," since I'm rather smug and confident right now. We are going to be travelling together for a while, so allow me to explain myself to you.

Let's start in 1942. You were still only a young boy at that time. The Nazis occupied your country and your father had gone to face them on the battlefield. He's proud of you, by the way. I wonder at how your species can exist in such a dichotomy—in one moment you are sitting peacefully drinking a coffee and in the next you could be, in the most futile fashion, fighting a seemingly insurmountable force for nothing more than to protect your land. It's fascinating. Regardless, I'll continue. By the time the Nazis had occupied your land, your father had already been taken prisoner in one of their camps and then escaped. You didn't know all the details of what was happening, but he somehow managed to return home. Those were difficult times for you. I'm certain you remember the grim scenes. Anyone who had been harbouring escapees paid a dear price. I can understand why you avoided talking about those days. How a child could not be damaged by the sight of their neighbours and friends hanging from trees while they tended to the family farm or walked home from school is unbelievable. You hid those scars quite well, I will admit. I can see them as clear as if they were physical, even in your current state. In that environment I was certain I would be taking you with me, young, but that hasn't ever been a deterrent. You didn't know I was there, watching. In fact, you didn't know much of what was happening.

You were sleeping on a bench in your house when the SS arrived. They came to search your house and a few others in the village. Fortunately for you, they sent a few soldiers who were more familiar with schnapps than the proper protocol for searching a house for an escapee or other undesirables. At the time, your father was hiding in the attic under some hay. They looked but didn't see him. That momentary lapse of diligence on their part was the difference between you leaving with me and remaining asleep. Your mother was braver than you might even know, and far more cunning than those Germans.

It wouldn't be until 1958 that I would have another chance. At this time, you were serving in the army, stationed in Montenegro. You and your friends were like a bunch of children. You probably remember that day pretty clearly. It was late autumn/ early winter, roughly seven degrees at sea level and probably twelve below at Bobotov Kuk, Mount Durmitor's peak. If not for the copper and bronze leaves on the trees, the slight breeze in the air and clear skies would have led one to believe it was a late spring morning. As your unit set out to the mountain that day, not a single one of you would have even imagined that you were being followed. You know, I don't like using words like *stalked,* because it gives such a negative and predatory view of what I do. There really is no necessity for you to like what I do, or me, but I can tell you beyond a shadow of a doubt I'm needed more than anyone else.

But I digress. Allow me to continue. So on your way up the mountain, you fools decided that you would again wager beer on who could reach altitude first before skiing back down. You were no higher than 500 metres and climbing the rock face at a point when your climbing acumen typically ensured you a free drink at the day's end. Although, on this day you decided that allowing your comrade to win would be the brotherly thing to do. You knew that you shouldn't have been climbing so slowly—it wasn't the way you typically climbed, and it was "anti-revolutionary," or whatever you said in those days. But even today, I can see that you haven't forgiven yourself for what you feel you did when you should have been ahead. This led to the rock I had left for you to use to lift yourself being grabbed by your friend. I know that the sound of that rock grinding against the rest of the cliff face followed by his fading and tortured screams found an eternal spot deep in the depths of your soul. That was your second little escape from my clutches.

I couldn't let that little setback on the mountain rattle my spirit, but I had bigger fish to fry. I decided the best thing for me to do was leave you alone for a little while. Actually, that in itself is one of the great advantages that I have over your kind. Your lifetimes are the single longest things you will do. Regardless of any other endeavor you undertake in your time, nothing will last longer than your life; that's it. It is the most tortured and prolonged thing you do, and as long as it feels for you, it's nothing more than a blink in time for me. A fleeting moment in which one missed opportunity is quickly replaced with another.

That next opportunity was gifted to me—unsurprisingly by you. You had moved to Austria and it was the '60s. Not only had the times in the world changed, but you had left a closed state and were now living in an open one. You lived a few good years there and were able to find some decent work in a mine. The work wasn't the best, but you were with a few people you knew and had a pretty good go of it while you were there. It was the latter half of winter that year, and you, as always, were working the mine, somehow the only person not covered in soot. You were tasked with something outside that day, which was unfortunate for me. I had ensured that one of the other workers would trigger a set of events that brought the mine crashing down on everyone. It was going to be an easy day: one act of God and weeks of less work for me. Yet again you managed to stay out of harm's way and were gone before the wheels were set in motion and my plan for things came to fruition. You said the next time you were underground would be when they buried you. I humbly concede that you stayed true to your word.

So now it was three times that you managed to cheat me; impressive, considering most are unable to even do it once. Interestingly, that is the kind of man you are: you have an innate ability to navigate through disaster and chaos and arrive to a peaceful place on the edge of the woods. There aren't too many who have that natural ability. Regardless, as I'm sure you see now, I am not one who can be cheated for very long. I will find your weaknesses and exploit what I need. It's nothing personal; it's just something that has to be done.

You know, beyond what I've already told you, I have been close to you so many times. I had decided that your unintentional ability to evade my efforts necessitated me observing you from time to time. Slowly I could see that you could manage to put yourself into positions which I, with little effort, should be able to take advantage of.

You must remember that summer when you and Ned were driving to Chicago in your Thunderbird, and you wanted to get there and make good time. I was riding in the back of your car as you two drove madly down the interstate, changing seats. Even a freeway paved as smooth as glass should have given you some type of issue, so I sat back and watched and waiting to bring both of you with me. I wasn't even trying that time, because even I believed it was beyond any realm of belief that you would walk out of that with your skin intact, and yet there you were, alive and well. I sometimes wondered if you had a sense that I was in the car with you that day. After your son was born, you sat with Ned and discussed how you could never talk about that day lest you give him any ideas. You can trust that I wasn't going to let chance control where things went forever. As I haven't let anyone before you slide by, I certainly wasn't going to be foiled by a village boy who made cheating me a lifetime hobby.

It was midsummer when we met again. Retirement hadn't slowed you down much; in fact, I would say you found your light in your golden years. Luckily for me, a lifetime of working in the dust of mines, the chemicals of an aerospace factory and, of course, let us not forget your smoking, had done enough to your lungs that all that was required was a little external intervention and time would, as it always does, take its course. Standing on the sixth tee, I am sure you thought nothing of that little cough. That again was me close to your side. As I observed you day after day and year after year, I realized that extraordinary situations were not what was needed. I had decided that it was best for me to use what tools you provided me to ensure my work could be done properly. Nothing more than the slightest of touches, and carcinogenic chemicals, which had been lying dormant, now actively invaded your lungs and intertwined with you to create what we have here today.

I want you to understand one thing: I completely understand the turmoil and pain that I have caused you in this process. But you must understand, I had given you four opportunities to allow me to do my work in a manner that would have ended things quickly, albeit terrifyingly. You failed to grasp the gift which I was so very generously giving you. Instead, you chose to cheat those opportunities and, rather than live fearing my eventual return, you scoffed at it. You thumbed your nose at me. This is an indignation which I cannot allow to continue without some type of recourse which befits the crime. I have brought many men so close to my side that they felt the air pushed aside from my cloak passing their face. So many of those men understood what I had done and lived their remaining days in fear, trying with a surplus of futility to escape my eventual return.

You did none of this. You continued to challenge me, and plainly spoke of the day we would meet again, as if it meant nothing to you. This is a feat that is neither commonplace nor easy, yet you, a simple village boy who travelled the world cheating me at every chance, did it with graceful ease. This is why I was left with no choice.

You've become somewhat of an obsession for me. Even when faced with my coming you've done almost nothing to show that I am near. This is why tonight I'm sitting here talking with you. I have been at the side of millions of hospital beds and almost always pass through casually, quietly calling on those I have come to collect. Rarely do I find a need to sit and talk with someone before we leave, but your continued defiance and resilience in my face has left me with little reason to not sit here and explain things to you. So tonight—again the transition time between late autumn and early winter—there are two things you must know. First, although I have put more effort into getting you here than I have for many others, I almost feel as if I am losing something, and my reward is not what it was meant to be.

Second, your calm demeanor precedes you, and although I brought you here in pain, you can now close your eyes and rest.

My Dearest Josephine

On Tue, Aug. 6, 2019, 11:42am Marcus <marcus191919@emailserver.com> wrote:

My dearest Josephine,

I'm so happy that we were able to spend yesterday together. There is so much more that I want to know about you, but hopefully we still have time for that. I wish that I had more to say while we were together but I have a nervous compulsion to be quiet when I'm around a woman. I find it much easier to write my thoughts down. It was actually quite nice to know that you are a quiet person as well.

I hope us finally meeting went as well for you as I perceived it to be.

I wait for your reply,
Marcus

***

On Fri, Aug. 9, 2019, 11:33am Marcus <marcus191919@emailserver.com> wrote:

Josephine,

Thank you for your reply. I know meeting for the first time is difficult and I was a little worried that you didn't have the same experience as I did, but I'm glad you did.

I almost forgot about the frogs at the pond! That was fantastic to be able to sit there and watch them catching flies. The weather was perfect to simply sit and enjoy the sounds and sun. Usually, you don't get to be that close to nature without it running away from you.

I'm glad you like the sweater I was wearing. I'm embarrassed to admit it, but I did buy it for our rendezvous. I felt like a giddy teenage girl going out shopping for our meeting. But on that note: seeing you was more than I could have imagined. When we met at the subway station I was able to pick you out of the crowd with no effort. Your beauty was a shining light on that street that caused everyone else to pale in comparison to the radiance you emanated. I know you said in your letter that you were nervous about how I would react to seeing you, but you have nothing to worry about.

And to answer you: of course I want to see you again! Thursday at the pond again?

Yours,
Marcus

***

On Sun, Aug. 25, 2019, 12:41pm Marcus <marcus191919@emailserver.com> wrote:

Dearest Josephine,

Seeing you yesterday was another glowing bright spot on an otherwise dim day for me. I'm glad we were able to see each other again. I don't know if you realize it, but your blue eyes carry all the warmth of a summer sky and the radiance of the sun.

I was hoping that we would exchange phone numbers and stop corresponding via email, but clearly, neither one of us thought of it. Maybe next time.

When you stepped into the pond and almost fell in, I apologize for laughing but your reaction was priceless. I would have considered letting go of your arm while we were both laughing but I thought better of it. Regardless, I can't help but believe that if you had fallen into the water it would have parted, not wanting to blemish your otherwise perfect looks.

In case you are wondering, yes that was the worst coffee I've ever had and under no circumstance did I pick it on purpose. You really were a trooper drinking it. I couldn't bring myself to tell you, but I was slowly spilling it as we were walking! It was truly horrible.

Maybe next time I can take you for a good coffee somewhere.

Yours truly,
Marcus

***

On Mon, Sep. 2, 2019, 1:02pm Marcus <marcus191919@emailserver.com> wrote:

Josephine,

I understand you don't have time to meet this week, there really is no need to apologize about it.

Also, I'm glad you didn't subject yourself to drinking that coffee either! I wonder if anybody walking behind us was wondering why we were slowly spilling coffee as we walked down the street.

I'm just in the middle of some things. I will write you again tomorrow and maybe we can arrange a time to meet up again.

Just tossing this out there . . . it might be easier if we had each other's phone numbers.

Marcus

***

On Mon, Sep. 2, 2019, 1:02pm Marcus <marcus191919@emailserver.com> wrote:

Hello again, Josephine,

If I remember correctly, you have Fridays off. Lunch at the pond? I'll let you bring the coffee this time.

Marcus

***

On Mon, Sep. 2, 2019, 4:32pm Marcus <marcus191919@emailserver.com> wrote:

Josephine,

Great. See you then.

Marcus.

***

On Sat, Sep. 7, 2019, 3:17pm Marcus <marcus191919@emailserver.com> wrote:

Josephine,

So I waited for you by the pond. You can't imagine how disappointed I am that you never made it, but I'm sure something came up. This probably could have been avoided via a quick text message if we exchanged numbers—you know, just saying.

Let me know when you can meet up again!

Marcus

***

On Tue, Sep. 10, 2019, 1:02pm Marcus <marcus191919@emailserver.com> wrote:

Josephine,

Is everything all right? It has been a few days since we last corresponded or saw each other. I don't want to fill your mailbox with emails, but I'm a little concerned to not hear from you. I decided to have a coffee at the pond today and thought about the last few times that we were there together. I know this is foolish, but I can't help but admit that I am becoming completely infatuated with you. I wait every day to see your radiant smile and warm eyes again. Please don't make me wait too long to hear from you again.

Please don't make me wait,
Marcus

***

On Sat, Sep. 14, 2019, 6:28pm Marcus <marcus191919@emailserver.com> wrote:

Josephine,

It has been a week since I last heard from you. I'm not sure what I did to make you stop speaking with me, but if you don't tell me there is nothing I can do to fix it. Please tell me what happened for you to decide that you no longer want me in your life. If something is wrong, let me know and I will do everything in my power to help you fix it or make what is wrong right.

I can be better,
Marcus

***

On Wed, Oct. 23, 2019, 9:45pm Marcus <marcus191919@emailserver.com> wrote:

Hello? Josephine??

It has been a month. Why did you tell me you wanted to see me again if you were going stop talking to me? Do you even realize how messed up this is? Why are you fucking with my mind? I'm sure that I saw you walking down the street yesterday. It was really nice of you to not wave back or say anything when I called across the street to you. Can you imagine how those poor people around me felt when I was yelling out to you? Who knows what they were thinking when I tried to get your attention. All you had to do was say hi and they wouldn't have felt so uncomfortable.

Just respond once so I know what's happening.

Marcus

***

On Wed, Oct. 24, 2019, 6:18pm Marcus <marcus191919@emailserver.com> wrote:

My Josephine,

I sat by the pond today. I was thinking about—wondering what has happened. The frogs were particularly active today and the warmth of the sun helped with the overall mood. I think you really would have liked how the flowers on the lilies shone in the afternoon sun. I had that horrible coffee again and had a little laugh about the first time we drank it and how we hid the fact that neither one of us wanted to admit to not actually drinking it.

Marcus

***

On Wed, Oct. 24, 2019, 11:09pm Marcus <marcus191919@emailserver.com> wrote:

Josephine, I'll keep writing till you hear me!

I can't take it anymore. I was at the pond again and all I could see was your ice-cold eyes and hear your voice taunting me on the wind. Who does that? I truly believe that you were there hiding in the trees, there's no other way I would have heard your vile voice. You know that day that you almost fell into the pond? Do you remember how I caught you and stopped you from falling in? Well, I want you to know that I now know that I should have let you fall in. Today while sitting there I could have thrown myself in the water just to have the chance to drown the thoughts of you. I hate every moment that your face is burned into my memory.

Marcus

***

On Sun, Sept. 7, 2019, 1:43am Marcus <marcus191919@emailserver.com> wrote:

Josephine,

Today I was out for a walk. I was drinking that coffee, that vile coffee you had me drink knowing that you hated it. Why else would you have bought it for me then left? Do you know the bridge over the river? You know the place, we walked past it before. I heard your voice there again. I don't know why the people walking by were looking at me. I can only assume that some of the women who crossed to the other side of the street were your friends that you sent to see what you have done to me. I guess they told you about how I wanted to throw you over the bridge into the river? Yeah, I told them all about it. Especially the blond one. Just ask her about it. I told her how I would grab you around the waist from behind and throw you over the guardrail into the river headfirst, right at the place where the rocks are, that way if the water doesn't drown you the rocks will break you enough so that you can't swim against the current. I'd cross the street just to watch you float away. That way I wouldn't have to see your nasty face or hear that voice on the wind anymore.

Why won't you talk to me?

Marcus

***

On Tues, Sept. 13, 2019, 6:02pm Marcus <marcus191919@emailserver.com> wrote:

Josephine,

I waited for you at the subway station today. I didn't even go to work. Do you realize what that could do for me at my job? I'm willing to lose my job to see you. I got there early, but you must have gone to work extra early today to avoid me. How did you know I was going to be there? I didn't tell anyone about it. I just wanted to talk to you, to find out what happened. But the longer you made me wait for you the angrier I became. Do you want to know what I could have done to you today? I stood there like a fool. People staring at me wondering why I wasn't getting on the train. I would have taken your beautiful brown hair in my hand. I would have gripped it between my fingers, twisted tightly so you couldn't pull away and I would have dragged you to the tracks. I would have held you there until the train went by. I would have lost my hand for you!

How many people would be willing to lose a limb for someone? Do you even know how much I love you? And you just leave me here to wait.

Why did you call me when I got home? The phone rang and nobody was there. Why did you do that? If you just gave me your number I could have called you and all of this could have been avoided. But you let me give you my number, didn't you? All you do is take from me. Everything I gave you I'd give you again.

Josephine, why did you do this to me?

Marcus

***

Dr. Eisman:

As you can see, I've attached a printout of a series of emails that were found by staff on Marcus Smith's email, which he left open. Marcus has clearly developed some sort of a delusion about a relationship with a woman who is entirely unknown to the staff at the facility. I've reviewed everything we have in Marcus's medical records and history and it has been determined that he has had no relationship with a woman named Josephine. I called his family and after speaking with them, they confirm Marcus has never known a woman by this name. The date stamps on the emails indicate that he wrote every email while a patient, and each was returned with a negative delivery notice. The increasingly violent desires detailed in the messages have become a serious cause for concern and he has since been transferred to a locked unit. I know you like to be briefed before patients are moved but I thought it was best to get things in motion quickly.

Dr. V

Tiberius Sardicus

By the time Flavius Justinianus Augustus came to power, I had already been serving under Flavius Belisarius as one of his Bucellarii. Clearly there was no better place that one such as myself could be fully integrated as a part of Roman society. It truly was the perfect fit. When Justin I died and Justinian took the throne of the Empire, my fortunes as a soldier and one seeking new hunting grounds significantly improved. General Belisarius was appointed as the commander of all Roman armies in the East, and with war against the Sassanids all but a foregone conclusion, this provided a great opportunity for the General and, more importantly, for myself.

All Romans were taught from childhood to fear the Strix, an owl of ill omen who fed on the flesh of humans. This is one of many Roman myths that had been created to explain the occurrences of dead Romans who had been clearly fed on in the darkness of the night. Some feared it may have been wolves, but as pack animals their presence was often known by the sound of their howls in the night. These people, the ones taken by the Strix, were killed and fed upon in the depths of the night and in silence. The nocturnal hunting of the owl was the only plausible explanation to your average Roman.

Naturally when I learned that we were, in fact, to face the Sassanids on the Empire's eastern frontier I had all my armour adorned with the image of the bird. Some in my unit took it as a bad omen destined to bring defeat and destruction to our cause. "You taunt the gods!" some would say. Others who had accepted Christianity claimed my armour's new design was an affront to their God, angels and saints. Despite the fear and anger infecting some of my unit, others saw it as a sign of the ferocity with which I would meet our enemies. Like the Strix, they said,

I would vanquish our enemies by tearing their flesh straight from their bones. Few actually would see and understand the true reason I carried the image on my armour; none would live to tell of its meaning.

At this time, I was known as Tiberius and I was a Roman soldier, and a part of the personal army of Flavius Belisarius, the Eastern Roman Empire's greatest general. I had built myself a reputation among other soldiers and the leadership, and most importantly with the General, as a fearless warrior who spared no enemies on the field of battle. It truly is a bitter irony of history that only the generals are remembered while the soldier's names who carried them to fame are forgotten in the sands of time. In none of the history books that speak of the Eastern Roman Empire will you read the name Tiberius of Sardica. What you must understand is that I don't carry any grievance with the General; in fact, the modern chronicles about this great man only dilute his character. He was a greater man and leader than the Emperor whom he served. Had I been the creator of the mosaic in the cathedral in Ravenna, Justinian would have stood to the right of Belisarius rather than the way it is. This was the character and the greatness of the General, forgotten in the West. Also forgotten is how his victories helped civilized Europe survive. But despite his greatness, one cannot forget the tide that carried him there. Do you truly believe he fought those battles against the Sassanids, the Visigoths, Ostrogoths, Lombards? He commanded the army, and the soldiers who stood loyal to the General stared our barbarian enemies in the eyes. But for all the mortal soldiers who valiantly fought for God and Empire, it took one without a soul, without remorse, to see the depth of fear which resided in the hearts of our enemies and to feed on this to help carry our army to victory. And that, in my assessment, is how the great General became the Titan he is.

I can understand that while reading this some may doubt my claims, but allow me to assuage them by recalling the events of the Battle of Dara. If nothing else, this will help you understand how I, and more importantly my talents, helped the Empire destroy its enemies and the General build his career. When the Sassanids arrived outside the walls of Dara, we found that the Imperial Army was outnumbered two to one by our enemy. They brought 50,000 men to the battle, where the Empire only provided the General a paltry 25,000. On the first day of the battle, both armies sent forward their chosen hero, a remnant of the ancient traditions. But these men were not Achilles nor Hector; they were nothing more than well-trained slaves, monkeys with weapons. Our monkey was the better fighter.

The second day of battle is where my fondest memories begin. The Bucellarii, of which I was attached to, faced the Sassanid Immortals. Immortals? These were but men with toys, and for this I would teach theses "immortals" what they were and nothing more. On the right flank of the battlefield the Immortals tried to push through the ditches outside the city walls, which our General had had the army build to fortify our position. Here I found my first engagement of the battle.

He was a young soldier no more than twenty-five. I found him crawling out of our defensive ditch, scratching at the dirt where the ditch's end met level ground. First his right hand scraped at the ground, digging into the grass and soil and slightly slipping back into the ditch, while his left hand quickly grabbed the ground opposite his right. Weighed down by his armour and weapons, his climb was painfully slow. Consumed by the chaos of the battlefield, he failed to notice my horse standing at the ditch's edge. What an illustration of the contrast of our two people right at that moment! The Sassanid barbarian crawling through the dirt weighed down by a fledgling's armour and insignificant weapons, while I, a symbol of Roman achievement, calmly watched him struggle, knowing that my superior Roman armour, weapons and tactics (even without immortal strength) ensured his demise. I commanded my horse, Tigris, to stomp his front hoof to the ground, and as if the beast's mind was connected to mine, he planted his foot right on the Sassanid's left hand. The barbarian screamed in pain and howled like an injured dog, and it was at this time he looked up and saw me calmly dismounting my horse.

His beady little brown eyes widened to their greatest extent—I think they would have popped out of his skull if they could. Half of his face may have been covered, but through his eyes I could see into the depths of his soul. All I could find in them was panic as he stared back at me. I am sure all he could see behind my eyes was death, a soulless emptiness. Both he and I knew that the last thing he would see or experience on this earth was me taking his life. Tigris held his ground and the Sassanid's left hand to the earth while the Sassanid flailed with his right hand in uncontrolled panic, reaching and grasping for any weapon he could get hold of in a pathetic attempt to prevent the inevitable. Amused, I watched as he flopped around on the ground like a fish plucked from the water, reaching for the spear still sheathed on his back. I removed the galea from my head, slowly placed it on the ground in front of Tigris, who slightly bowed as if to acknowledge my intent. I turned by my right shoulder and faced the Sassanid still reeling in pain and grabbing at his spear. His right hand held above his head had just taken hold of the spear's shaft, a little glimmer of hope in his final moments on earth. I reached down, held his right arm in my left hand and leaned my head beside his. "Today, you feed the Strix," I calmly told him. I squeezed his right arm until his ulna and radius popped and cracked, snapping like brittle twigs. This renewed his screams of pain, and when I could feel that his bones were completely shattered I dug my fingers into his flesh and pulled his forearm apart. Blood flowed out of his fresh wounds like water through a breached dam, and I pulled his severed forearm away and watched as his flesh stretched until it separated from its base. As the skin peeled apart, the sound reminded me of wet linen being torn, and his blood splattered into his eyes and onto my arm. His howls of pain were replaced by the silence of shock at what was happening to him. He watched in disbelief as I took his severed arm to my mouth and drank his blood, which poured out unreservedly. While drinking, I raised my sword above my head and cleaved his skull in two. He was silenced.

You must remember this all happened during the course of the battle. I now had to find my next victim.

Tigris and I moved forward through the Immortal's ranks and they fell to our sides, a tide of fallen soldiers washing away like the rapids of a river smashing on the rocks. We forged ahead, breaching our enemy's ranks. I hacked Sassanid arms from torsos and the "immortals" fell to the ground. Tigris crushed their skulls under the weight of his hooves. I looked down at one point to witness a fallen Sassanid's head crushed under Tigris's hoof. After losing his right arm to my sword, the barbarian fell to his back and could only look up wide-eyed as

Tigris's hind leg crushed his face into the back of his skull.

The following day was spent cleaning the Sassanid filth off of my trusted companion's legs. We, the Roman Bucellarii, were the rocks upon which the General's army was built. As the Immortals fell to our sides, so did the Sassanids' will to fight. The battle raged for the duration of this second day, and with each passing hour the numbers of Sassanids whose lives I took grew in number.

One of the Sassanid leaders, Baresmanas, was killed along with 5,000 of his men when they attacked our position. I will never know with one-hundred-percent certainty what Baresmanas's motivation was. Did he intend to smash his floundering army against the tide of our forces? But it is my wholehearted belief that this was a desperate attempt at slowing our inevitable victory. There was no way that even within his fragile Sassanid mind that he could have believed this could have improved their fortunes. The battle was decided before it was even fought, before even their army set forth to assault our Empire.

It was in this skirmish that I was left with little choice but to take the life of a fellow Roman. In this moment I again found myself alone, even while in the presence of so many others. This was a moment that separated me from every other Roman I stood with. The Sassanid pushed into our lines, attempting to pursue our cavalry, and their soldiers, along with Baresmanas, found themselves trapped within our lines with no route to escape. It was little more than a slaughter, and it was in this chaotic bloodbath that I arrogantly took the opportunity to feed on Sassanid flesh again.

As we hacked our way through their ranks, the panicked Sassanids practically killed each other in an attempt to escape our swords. In this melee I took hold of a Sassanid soldier who, in the confusion, dropped his weapons and clawed at the fallen around him to get away. He didn't even see me coming. I approached him from behind and grabbed him on the outside of his shoulders, pulling him back toward me. I could feel the adrenalin coursing through my veins as I dug my teeth into his neck. He screamed, probably not even knowing what was attacking him. I bit down so hard that the incisors from the top of my mouth and jaw snapped together in the middle of his muscle. I tore the flesh and muscle off his neck and shoulder, and the blood from his carotid artery sprayed with enough force to make his wound seem like the spout of a fountain from a city centre. The smell of the blood as it rushed past my face only intensified my hunger for more human flesh. My eyes rolled back in my head as I took another bite out of this unknown man, and my teeth this time scraped his now exposed collar bone. By this time, he was certainly dead.

I swallowed this last taste of flesh and saw to my right a fellow Roman who had been sprayed with the blood of this Sassanid, causing him to look to his left in time to observe me taking another bite. We stood motionless, staring at each other. The chaos of the battle must have faded into the background for him. He was a battle-hardened soldier, yet as he stood there staring at me, blood covering my face and pieces of Sassanid flesh hanging from my mouth dripping with blood, he became as pale as a ghost. Every ounce of blood in this man's body drained from his skin and he froze in time, a statue paralyzed by the shock of what he had just seen. I cleaned the Sassanid flesh from my teeth and motioned with a finger over my lips for him to be silent. The man nodded slowly, still staring at me, this monster that hours earlier he believed to be a fellow Roman, a brother-in-arms. I unsheathed my sword and motioned for us to continue the fight. And as if suddenly woken from a deep sleep, he came to and continued to fight.

The melee took 5,000 Sassanid lives, yet it is that one insignificant soldier's life that I took which ran the risk of exposing me to the rest of the army, and more importantly to the General. That night as our men celebrated our victory over the Sassanids, I knew I would have to take the life of one of my fellow Bucellarii.

From the moment the battle ended and on through the night, I followed his every movement. I watched him enter a little tavern in the city, a typical place where you would find all the city's vagabonds, soldiers, and whores. He guzzled wine, no doubt in an attempt to temporarily forget what he had seen, and when he paid for a whore and took her to a room above the tavern, I had my opportunity to silence him. As they took to their room, I sat perched on the ledge outside their window and waited. I knew I would be taking his life in short time, so I decided I could wait a few minutes to allow him one last moment of pleasure. The room went silent as both lay quietly on the bed.

By the time they noticed my presence in the room, it was too late for either of them to make a noise. I stood on the bed and grasped their throats in my hands and squeezed, feeling them popping and crackling under the pressure. I loosened my grip on the whore to allow myself a meal before departing the room, but my fellow Bucellarii's throat collapsed under the pressure and I felt my fingers rip through his flesh as my fingertips made contact behind his throat. Blood splattered across the bed, the walls and the whore's face. His body went limp in my hand and all the colour drained from his face. Still in shock, she didn't struggle against me, and when I exposed my teeth ready to feed, a look of defeat come over her. As my incisors pierced the skin on her neck and her blood flowed across my tongue and filled the inside of my mouth, the limpness that I felt in her muscles was that of relaxation and concession before eventual death. Despite the commotion and noise radiating from the tavern and streets below, the room in which I stood was a vacuum of silence.

After Dara and the killing of my brother-in-arms, I took leave of the army and returned to my homestead in Sardica. I had a small cottage in the forest outside of the city walls. My time in Dara had only solidified my knowledge that I couldn't fully integrate into Roman society, or into a fraternity such as Belisarius's Bucellarii. My ability to take the lives of our enemies with almost mechanical efficiency wasn't enough to overcome the fact that not only was I not a Roman, but other than the armour and uniform I wore I was not like the men I fought beside. My only option was to return to Sardica and continue my existence where it began.

I Feed the Crow

The progression of events surrounding the last number of weeks don't seem to have a logical flow or starting place. Despite an attempt to track what has happened and where I am, my ability to concretely track the progression of time seems to have dwindled, but what I can say is that everything seemed to happen on a Thursday in late autumn some weeks ago—if "happened" is the best way to describe it. I woke up around eight forty-five in the morning. The house was unusually quiet, but I thought nothing of it and went through my normal routine, after which I went downstairs. I found that there was nobody home. Usually my girlfriend, Evalyn, who prefers the nostalgic feel of radio broadcasts over television news, would leave the radio on as a way of breaking the silence of an otherwise empty house. It was always nice to have the radio playing over the monotonous sound of electricity flowing through household appliances. But that Thursday there was no radio broadcast, no music to fill the air, the radio was off and there was nothing but silence. I called out to my family, but nobody responded. The frying pan was on the stove as if someone was about to make breakfast, but there was nothing taken out of the fridge or on the counter. Despite this, I wasn't concerned, as it wouldn't be beyond the realm of possibility that they went out for the morning and left me to sleep. *Fantastic,* I thought. *Finally, some silence and alone time.* I sat down to watch television, started flicking through channels, but found that none were broadcasting. News channels: nothing. Sports channels: again nothing. Children's channels: still nothing. The television worked, but none of the channels did. It was weird, and a little bit eerie. I walked over to our front bay window and looked out to our street, which usually had some type of activity, particularly during the Christmas season. Again, there was nothing but silence.

I grabbed my coat and boots and headed outside to see if I could find somebody around. Both of our cars were still home, so everybody must have left on foot, I surmised. I walked from our front step to the cars to check if they were locked. All I could hear was the crunching of hardened snow beneath my feet, and each step echoed in my ears as if there were no other sounds in the world. Pulling on the handles of the car doors, I could hear that the hinges were somewhat corroded and more audible than usual. Looking around, I realized that everybody's cars were home and there were no other sounds. It was complete silence except the buzzing of electricity flowing through the power lines. I stood still for a good two minutes, the only sound the power lines, a constant low buzzing, and the sound of my breathing. My breath condensed in the cold air, flowing up into my line of sight, the only movement.

After a few minutes in the cold, I returned to my house to gather my thoughts. It took me a while to figure it out, but for some reason I still do not understand, everybody in the neighbourhood was gone. Everything was gone. People, animals, everything. But there was still power and everything was working . . . ish. None of the channels were broadcasting, but the television worked and I could channel surf through static and white noise, and although there was nobody around there was still electricity. This led me to the belief that there must be somebody somewhere, if the power was still on. I spent the better part of the first day sitting in the house trying to understand what was going on, and what could have possibly happened to everyone.

It would have been around eight o'clock. that first night when I started to come to the realization that I had spent the entire day doing whatever I wanted, with nobody bothering me, on my schedule and at my discretion. Evalyn and the kids had been gone all day, something I wasn't at all familiar with, and to my best recollection the last time I can truly say I was alone was before the kids, maybe even before Evelyn and I got together. Eight, ten years? I can't be sure anymore. There was a peaceful, calm, and ever-present silence. I always enjoyed being alone, but it was something that became harder and harder to achieve as time went on. But now, for whatever reason, I finally had what I had always wanted, and foolishly spent the whole day sedentary wondering where everyone was. It was complete idiocy for me to waste the day like that; I had no idea what was going on or how long I would be alone. Time was of the essence, and I finally decided that I would have an early night and get going the next morning, start to explore, figure out what had happened and try to determine how long I would be alone. If I was still alone.

The next morning, I woke up around six thirty and it was still dark out. I listened and couldn't hear anything, which admittedly wasn't so odd at that hour in our house. I quietly crept around the house to ensure that I was still alone, and my excitement multiplied with every step that I realized I was. The first thing I did was get some music playing (mp3s, since, much like television, nothing was broadcasting on the radio) and started to make breakfast. Eggs, bacon, toast, black coffee and a screw-it-all attitude was my breakfast that day. I sat on the widow's wharf above our front door, which until this day I always thought was a waste of space, and watched the sun rise over our neighbourhood. I was able to sit with my thoughts and watch the sun rise above the roof- and treetops to take its place in the sky. The only sound offsetting the silence was the buzzing of the power lines, something that I thought I would be able to get used to.

After the sun was up, I prepared myself to explore the neighbourhood and see who or what was around. I grabbed my white ski jacket and some other winter clothes—hat, gloves and so on. I also brought a backpack with some food and drinks in it, not knowing how long I'd be out and if I would be able to get something to eat or drink anywhere. With that, I started out.

I headed south from my house down our street toward the downtown. I walked directly down the middle of the street and could hear nothing other than my footsteps. I checked a few houses, and all of them were empty. It seems wherever my family went was the same place everyone else in the neighbourhood did.

I started walking east on a cross street and heard a fluttering of wings behind me. I spun around quickly, startled by the sound, and sitting on the top of one of the electrical posts was a crow. I stood there staring at it for a couple seconds as it stared back at me. It bobbed its head up and down and cocked it left and right, seemingly measuring up what I was and figuring out why I was walking down the street. After a few moments of staring at each other, he cawed and the sound of his voice shattered the silence of the street and echoed, his call reverberating through the silent emptiness.

"Well, hello to you too," I responded. "You're more than welcome to come with me if you want. I assume you are also alone?" The crow cawed again. "Well, let's go," I said. I turned around and continued walking east. Every few seconds I heard the fluttering of the bird's wings. The first few times I looked back to see that he was jumping from the top of one electrical pole to the next. This continued for the whole walk.

When I reached the downtown commercial area of the city, I heard the crow caw and flutter his wings before coming to rest on a lower light post. As you enter the old commercial district of the city from the newer suburban area, the style of the light posts changes to a more artistic, antique look. The lights in this part of town look more like the candlelit lamps of the nineteenth century than the generic concrete light poles characteristic of the twentieth-century suburban streets which dominate the majority of the city. It was probably one of my favourite places in the city: the shops, cafés and nostalgic appearance always appealed to me. I continued walking into the downtown, and after a few moments I stopped noticing that I hadn't heard the fluttering of my companion's wings. Looking back, I could see that he was sitting on the first of the downtown light posts, bouncing his head up and down. "Are you coming?" I called out to the bird. He sat there looking at me in a crooked manner, not leaving his perch. "Well, that's fine, you wait there, and I'll see what I can find in here."

The majority of the stores were still locked. It appeared that nobody had been in them for a little while. I was able to find a coffee place that was unlocked and grabbed some food for myself and bread for the crow—I expected that he would be waiting for me. I continued walking the downtown streets for a while longer and found that the majority of doors were locked and unattended, but everything was empty and clearly nobody had been around for at the very least a couple of days. I started back toward home, and as the edge of the downtown came into view I saw it sitting on its perch on the light post. The bird must have seen me because it began to bounce and caw, presumably at the sight of me. Upon getting close enough I started speaking with him again.

"Did you think I wasn't going to come back for you? Well, not to worry, I brought something for you as well." I threw the bread on the road beside me and the crow jumped down, grabbed a few little pieces and flew back up to the top of the electrical post. We continued this way all the way back to my house. As I walked up my street, I was relieved to see the sight of my house; after a whole day of walking my feet were tired and I really needed a warm fire and hot coffee.

The bird stopped at the end of my street and watched me from the top of a stop sign. I looked back and asked, "Are you planning to wait there all night? I have more to feed you at my house if you like." The bird just cawed and stood on the sign, staring at me and cocking its head back and forth. "Suit yourself." I continued home, made a fire and a meal and enjoyed a good book over a drink before eventually falling asleep.

The following day I made for another part of town, and the bird again followed me, jumping from light post to light post, cawing in response to my many random questions. My half-hearted one-way conversation continued with the bird everywhere we walked, and I imagined its sporadic cawing as its interjections and contributions. When I would reach where I had decided to go, the bird would wait outside before following me nearly all the way home. That pretty much completed my first week. It was after that when I thought it would be best to write all this down. I was able to find a store that was open and grabbed this diary to write my thoughts in. I didn't trust that I would always be able to use my laptop, so I thought it better to do it the old-fashioned way.

My fickle nature has had the best of me and it has been a few weeks since I wrote anything, so I thought I would update what I've been doing with my time. At this point,

I have pretty much explored the entire city and found that, other than me and the bird, everything is empty of life. I'm left with the belief that something must have happened, but I still have no idea what that could have been. I can't remember now when I realized it or how it dawned upon me, but one morning while I was sipping my coffee I came to the realization that I had neither worried or thought about where my family was. My mind was continually filled with thoughts of where to explore next, and whether the bird would follow me again.

As it turned out, my friend regularly accompanied me on my exploratory walks. Despite having traversed the majority of the city, I continue my daily walks and exploration, but now it's becoming more out of habit and to see if the crow will continue to follow me than to find anything new. I decided one day to go downtown again, just to kill time. The cafés, shops and nostalgic look are beginning to lose their lustre. I have always found it pleasant to visit a café and read a book or something similar, but with nobody to discuss the book with it starts to become somewhat stale. Although, with nothing else to do, I thought it no worse to be alone in the café than at home.

On this day, like every one before it, my friend was waiting for me at the crossroad of my street and the next. Much like the first day when I was leaving the downtown, upon seeing me the crow began to bounce on his perch and caw at me. "I'm coming, I'm coming, relax," I called back. "Impatient today, are we?" Once I reached the crossroad where he was waiting, I started walking east and the crow fluttered along with me from post to post.

Reaching the downtown commercial area, I expected my companion to take his place on the first light post, but, to my surprise, he followed me in. "Oh, so you've decided to finally join me, have you?" I asked. The bird just cawed and continued to jump from post to post as I walked. We came to a pet store which, having checked on it a few occasions previously, I knew was locked. I stood in front of the window of the store thinking for a few moments, the bird perched on a light post behind me. I looked back at him.

"What do you think, should I?" With a crooked stare, the bird stood there quietly. "Well, I'm not going to be the one eating the seeds, so if you want them let me know," I said. The bird shifted his crooked look from right to left, still silent. I decided that it didn't really make a difference, since there was nobody else around, and I picked up a garbage can on the street and threw it through the window of the store. The shattering of glass sounded like an explosion through the otherwise silent street. The bird cawed approvingly and jumped back and forth between two light posts in front of the store. I retrieved what I wanted to get for my friend and we continued on our walk through the downtown streets. I came to the same café I had been coming to when I came down here alone. I went inside and made myself a coffee and something small to eat, then took a seat beside the fireplace. I wasn't even able to start reading before I heard a rapping on the window. I could see the crow tapping his beak on it, pausing for a moment to stare at me, then continuing. I opened the door and the bird bounced in and perched himself on a chair close to the fire where I was sitting.

The walk back home was much like the walk to the café. The bird jumped from post to post, only fluttering to the ground to pick up some of the seeds I left on the ground to feed him, before returning up to the posts from where he came. Every so often he would caw and break the silence. "You know, I can't help but think you are trying to remind me of how quiet it is when you caw like that," I told him. The bird looked at me and bounced up and down on his post. Once we got to my street, it took its place on the stop sign and watched me walk away. It was nice to get home, and I made a fire and settled in for the night.

Today, I woke up in a rather morose mood. I hadn't been out much in the last couple days and thought that the crow may possibly have left rather than waiting for me at the end of the street again. Regardless, I puttered around the house for about an hour before deciding that I needed to make something to eat. While in the kitchen making a coffee and waiting for my food to heat up, I thought about the monotony of being in my home the last few days. Having pretty much read every book we have and with nothing on TV, I've started to become frustrated with being alone. I seem to be the only person in the world, and the life that I had previously had, often filled with conversations with my girlfriend and children's activities, seems like a distant dream.

Their absence isn't what has put me in this mood, but rather my lack of fully grasping the opportunity which my solitude has afforded me.

I continued my thoughts as I prepared my meal, and just as I sat down to eat my food, which didn't seem very appetizing, I heard a tapping on the kitchen window. The crow was on the windowsill giving me a crooked look. I couldn't believe what I was seeing: the damn bird found where I live and was waiting for me outside. It tapped on the window, just as it did at the café, pausing to look at me before continuing to tap. I opened the window and the crow jumped into the kitchen. It hopped around the floor for a minute before perching itself on a chair. Not knowing what else to do, I ate my breakfast with the crow sitting across from me, quietly watching.

After breakfast, I left the house with no particular direction in mind. The weather wasn't bad, so I grabbed a lighter coat, the grey one. I didn't really feel I needed a hat, but I still threw one in my backpack. I have made a habit of always bringing my backpack with me when I go anywhere, in the event I find something that I want to bring home with me. I walked and randomly threw seeds down for the crow, and every couple power poles he would jump down and feed on the seeds then return to the post tops.

I have decided that I have had enough of home for now. There is nothing there and

I need to be somewhere else. So today I left from home with my companion and walked to a different neighbourhood where I didn't know anyone. I walked from house to house, the crow following. I walked up to each house and looked in through the windows and doors to see if they had what I wanted. I don't know how many hours had passed, but dusk was approaching and I was starting to run out of time to make my decision. I finally decided on a small bungalow at the corner of some street—I didn't even know what street I was on at this point, not that it matters. Inside the house was a fireplace, lots of canned food in the kitchen and books and movies which will keep me occupied while I'm here. I waited for the crow to come in, but it just bounced around the front yard cawing and didn't come into the house. I threw some seeds down for it and sat outside on the doorstep to see what it would do, but not wanting to spend the entire night outside I went in and left him out in the yard. He continued to caw for a few more hours, but eventually quieted down when I started watching movies.

Some time has again passed since I last wrote anything, and I thought it best that I put down some thoughts on paper. Spring is around the corner and the weather is starting to get better. I left the bungalow a while ago, and since then I haven't really stayed in any one place for longer than two nights. I can't seem to find any place that I enjoy anymore. Being alone is beginning to wear on me. I was happy at first when I realized that there were no people around, but as time has passed the feeling of being alone has begun to weigh heavier on me. The only thing that I can seem to be certain of is the crow, which is still following me around. It has taken to following me into any house or apartment that I decide to stay in and no longer hops on the power or light poles when we walk the city. He follows right beside me, bouncing along the street. I don't even bother to speak with him anymore. There really isn't anything to say.

The farther I walk, the more places I stay at, the more he follows me closely. We travel and find whatever we can to feed him and continue our travels together. All I have now is my time with the crow. All the crow has is what I feed him.

THE STORY OF MIROSLAV PEK

This is the story of one Miroslav Pek. Mr. Pek was not a man who inspired greatness, yet neither was he a man who invited pity. It would not be unusual if Miroslav Pek traversed a day without ever being noticed. He wore simple clothes and had a plain haircut. To say there was nothing regarding Mr. Pek's appearance that warranted retention in one's memory would be less a statement of scorn and more a statement of mere fact. He inhabited a simple apartment on a regular street in an old part of town. Every morning, as with the morning we speak of here, Miroslav would walk to a small café a short distance from his apartment, buy a coffee and sit on the patio which faced a small urban park and start his day.

Today, as he arrived at the café, he looked over the outside seating, which sat on a small cobblestone patio. Six small tables, each with two wrought-iron bistro chairs, filled the area. Miroslav gladly observed that none of the tables were occupied. The morning patrons at this café rarely stayed to have their drinks. With the exception of Miroslav Pek, the morning patrons were in the midst of their daily rush to get to work. This allowed Miroslav to sit alone on the cobblestone patio and contemplate all the things that a man like him contemplates. Miroslav opened the door to the café, glass with a painted black steel handle, which swung in toward the interior. On the door was written the café's name and hours of operation. Miroslav noticed how even at this early hour the glass of the door was riddled with the palm and arm prints of previous patrons who were seemingly in too much of a rush to use the handle provided, thus leaving their greasy marks on the glass. As he entered, not a single person looked up or turned to look at Miroslav. All were clearly too preoccupied with their own thoughts to notice an otherwise unnoticeable man. Miroslav walked up to the counter and waited his turn to order. The counter was wooden, with a hand engraving of a map of Central and South America, perhaps to indicate the geographic locations where they purchased their coffee beans. He looked at the items sitting on the counter: plates of pastries covered with glass and a wooden hand-painted sign he always enjoyed, which read: UNATTENDED CHILDREN WILL BE GIVEN ESPRESSO AND A PUPPY THEN RETURNED TO THEIR PARENTS.

"Two seventy-five," he heard from the girl at the counter.

"Excuse me?" Miroslav asked.

"Oh, I'm sorry," she said. "I just thought you wanted your usual."

"My usual?" Miroslav asked, perplexed.

"Yeah, a medium Americano, no milk, no sugar, half and inch from the rim," the girl said, smiling at Miroslav.

He could hardly believe what he had heard. Miroslav had been coming to this café for the better part of four years, and at no point in that time had anyone remembered his order. Except now, Veronica knew his order and seemingly knew who he was. Miroslav knew who Veronica was—he would watch her from his table on the cobblestone patio, making sure to remember her name as it was written on her nametag. Not that Miroslav would ever engage Veronica in conversation; that isn't what a man like Miroslav Pek does. Miroslav had always found Veronica to be very attractive. She was twenty years old, five feet three inches tall, shorter than Miroslav by a head. She had slightly longer than shoulder-length light brown hair, blue eyes, and fair skin that freckled in the summer months. She wore thick-framed black glasses, which Miroslav thought gave her a librarian's look.

"I'm sorry if you wanted something else," Veronica said.

"No, no, that's exactly how I like it," Miroslav responded, handing her the money.

She smiled at him and went about making his drink. Miroslav watched her intently.

"I can bring it out to you on the patio if you like. It's no problem."

He smiled, nodded and headed to out to his regular table facing the park.

He had only been sitting a minute when Veronica arrived with his coffee. "Here you go. I hope you enjoy. By the way, my name is Veronica."

"Thank you. Miroslav," he responded.

Miroslav sat and contemplated the things that a man like him contemplates.

Miroslav passed the rest of his day largely unnoticed, except through his early morning encounter with Veronica. Nighttime came and he retired to his apartment. Lying in his bed, he began to relax and ready for sleep when his calm was disrupted by chirping crickets outside his window. Miroslav tossed and turned in his bed, but the longer he stayed awake the less he could relax and the more the shrill creaking penetrated into his mind.

At no later than three in the morning he sat up, still haunted by the chirping insects. Staring into the darkness of his room, he thought, *It was her.*

The chirping grew shriller, penetrating deeper into the depths of his mind. *They've never kept me awake before,* Miroslav thought, *and after this morning, here they are.* Out of bed now, Miroslav paced his room.

"Why?" he asked aloud. "What could have possessed her to send these creatures to torment me?" Speaking only to himself, Miroslav continued, "Today she speaks to me, brings me my coffee. These unprovoked acts of kindness. All to distract me from her true intentions. That deceptive smile . . . what devilish soul does she hide behind her eyes?" This mad discourse continued through the night. By the time the sun began to rise, Miroslav was sitting silently on the edge of his bed, quietly staring out his window.

"It is six o'clock now. The café must be opening. That witch and she-devil must be there waiting to taunt me again, with her disingenuous smile and her lack of kindness. I mustn't be tired when I arrive. I can't let her know it worked."

Miroslav made his way to the café. As he arrived, he looked to the cobblestone patio and observed, as always, that nobody was occupying the bistro chairs facing the park. He opened the front door, again noticing the handprints left by people unable or unwilling to use the handles, and walked in. To his surprise, standing behind the wooden counter, engraved with a map of Central and South America, was a male, not the she-devil he was expecting.

Despite this, Miroslav approached the counter and made his regular order. The man serving him seemed to hardly notice his existence except for the fact he had money in his hand for the coffee. He seemed to look past Miroslav to the other patrons, something Miroslav was accustomed to. Upon receiving his coffee, Miroslav politely asked the barista where Veronica was.

"Oh, she's closing tonight, bro. Next."

Miroslav took his place on the cobblestone patio and contemplated the things a man like him contemplates.

Of course she is working tonight. She must be sleeping from her night of watching me. She must have brought the crickets to me and watched how I was tormented by their chirping. And now she sleeps. She knew I would be here in the morning to show her I wasn't tired, that I wasn't tortured by her crickets. She comfortably sleeps while I sit here.

At midnight, Veronica finished closing the café, locked the door and began to walk home. The area was at this hour void of pedestrian or vehicular traffic, yet still polluted with the noise of town. These two facts in concert worked well with the places decided upon earlier in the day by Miroslav Pek.

Veronica had barely walked a few steps from the café when she felt someone grab her from behind and a sharp pain in the back of her head. Instantly, she felt her legs give way and all went black.

She woke sometime later lying on the ground, her hands and feet bound and her mouth gagged with some sort of rag and tape. As her vision cleared, she saw Miroslav sitting over her.

"Oh, so we have decided to wake up, have we?" Miroslav asked.

Veronica tried to struggle against her bindings, but as soon as she moved she felt Miroslav kick her in the side of chest.

"There really is no point in fighting. I know it was you," Miroslav said.

Veronica stared at him blankly, paralyzed with terror at this otherwise unassuming man. He stood over her, staring directly with an emptiness that made her feel he was looking at nothing before him.

"You sent the crickets!" Miroslav yelled.

Veronica, now crying, shook her head in protest.

"Don't lie to me, don't you even lie to me. I know it was you. There were never crickets there, then the day you see me, notice me, smile at me, crickets torment me at night." Miroslav's voice cracked as he spoke. "You enjoyed your fun; you watched my torment. You lied to me with your feigned kindness."

Miroslav turned and picked up a small bag. "I collected these for you today." He emptied the contents of the small bag onto Veronica's head.

She screamed into her gag as dozens of crickets poured onto her. She shook herself violently on the ground, attempting to shake the insects off her face and out of her hair. When she opened her eyes, she saw Miroslav kneeling beside her with a knife in hand. Veronica felt the knife stab her abdomen the first three times, after which she became numb to all feeling.

The following morning, Miroslav returned to the café. As he approached, he saw a police car parked on the street in front. He passed the café and looked at the cobblestone patio and smiled upon seeing it again unoccupied. He opened the door, saw the handprints of various patrons on the glass and walked in. This morning was unusually busy, as police officers seemed to be speaking with all the regular patrons.

Miroslav approached the wooden counter, with a hand engraving of a map of Central and South America, and ordered his regular coffee. While waiting for his drink to be prepared, Miroslav listened as a police officer spoke with the man who served him yesterday.

"So, can you think of anyone, maybe someone who is a regular here, who may have known her?" the police officer asked.

"No. She didn't really socialize with any of our regulars. Corporate types, not really her thing."

"Nobody ever came looking for her?"

"Not that I can think of. Like I said, her friends weren't our customers."

Miroslav took his coffee: Americano, no milk, no sugar, filled half and inch from the rim. He proceeded to exit the café and go the patio, sit at his spot on the cobblestone patio, smile, and contemplate the things a man like Miroslav Pek contemplates.

The Wolf's Hair

I returned home with my wife for a visit with family after working abroad. Old-world custom had bound us to spend the first few days of the trip visiting extended family on a couple-day crusade to drink coffee at as many houses as we could in as short a time as possible. The trappings of modern society and the reality of a constantly changing economy had served to push some members of the family to opposite corners of the country, thus alleviating us of a couple of afternoon coffees with people I hadn't seen or spoken with for longer than I had been gone.

As a result, I was now afforded extra time to fulfill a commitment I had made to my mother on previous trips home. Often the discussion of visiting the cemetery where my grandparents had been buried was brought up, and for no good reason I was always able to divert the discussion and idea away and postpone a visit there. On this occasion, it seemed that my ambivalence to the idea had been circumvented by happenstance. With a lack of living relatives to visit and the timing of my trip being in the week preceding Saint Dimitri, which marked the approaching Saturday as a memorial day, or day of the dead on our religious calendar, I knew that my commitments had been secured for a trip of memorial observance.

That Saturday approached with a menacing speed, the nights preceding it blurred through the copious consumption of brandy and vodka and the days passed in the darkness of a deathly sleep. I would claim fatigue from my travels and the taxing visitation with family previously described, but I would be in a state of delusion if I failed to acknowledge the leading role that drink played in this blurred timeline. Among the unwelcome events of the passing days, I spent a great deal of time diverting discussion away from the happenings of my personal life and leisure time, a topic which as a child I felt compelled to keep private, and more so now as I no longer answered to any paternal figure on a daily basis.

Saturday morning was welcomed by the singing of blue jays and the brightness of a clear sunny sky. The beauty of this warm autumn morning was only contrasted by the macabre appearance of the bare branches of an oak tree visible through my bedroom window. Having grown up in my parents' house with this oak, I watched as the branches pushed up against my window like the fragile bony fingers of an aged decrepit man grasping for the youthful life that had long since passed him by. In much the same manner, the dark silence of death enveloped both the elderly man and the tree that once bore enough leaves to provide comfort and shade from the scorching heat of the summer sun.

After a pleasant and filling coffee and breakfast, my wife, my mother and I departed for the cemetery. It seemed a twist of fate that on such a bright and sunny morning we would be destined to travel to a place of sorrow and darkness. The road to the cemetery was lined with mature oak and maple trees. By their size, it was obvious that they had seen more time pass than most who resided in the neighbourhoods in which they now stood. The road and sidewalks were covered in leaves, providing a mosaic of red and yellow to be travelled on. The contrast of brightness on the ground to the desolation of the uppermost reaches of the trees was a sobering reminder of the cycle of life, which moves forward unhindered by all attempts by humanity to stop or understand it.

We drove into the cemetery though the main gate and were greeted with a sea of headstones protruding from the earth, each a varying shade of monotonous gray, and each a reminder that there is no natural escape from their clutches. Small paths used simultaneously as walking paths and roadways criss-crossed the cemetery, each branching off the last with no visible organization or particular uniformity. All the paths eventually reconnected with the main roadway that led us through the gate, but from our current perspective each just seemed to fade away between the endless waves of grave markers and headstones.

We veered to the left at a time when I expected we would be going right, but not having been here in years I accepted that my memory of the layout of the cemetery was suspect, at best. We finally came to a stop in front of a black hearse, which was blocking the way. Standing outside the vehicle was my aunt and uncle, and a family friend and his wife whom I hadn't seen or spoken with in what felt like a lifetime.

We exchanged pleasantries and I questioned why we were in this area of the cemetery, and if my memory had misled me as to the location of my grandparents' resting place. Everyone assured me that my memory hadn't misled me, but for today's purposes we needed to be here. The cryptic nature of everyone's response left me somewhat confused, although for the sake of expediting proceedings I chose not to push the issue, as there would be time after the initial ceremonial practices of visiting the grave and lighting candles to discuss such matters. Regardless, it all seemed trivial to me at this point.

My Uncle Stan and our friend Thomas removed from the hearse a particularly ornate sarcophagus. The lid was engraved with an effigy of a man lying on his back, legs side by side and arms crossed on his chest. The face of the man was grotesque and appeared to be not human, carrying instead the appearance of some type of a monster. Its engraved hair was long and draped over the shoulders, and its forehead was wrinkled with large eyebrows made to appear bushy and furrowed at the ends. The eyes, although open, were large and empty with no cornea or pupil showing. I was left with the impression that the eyes were intentionally left this way. The creature's nose was large and wrinkled with the nostrils flared. And its mouth, although closed, revealed two fangs protruding menacingly over the lower lip. With my curiosity at its peak, I pressed for answers as to why we were in possession of such a thing. I failed to remember any ceremonial practice or custom that would have necessitated the need for it. Thomas's wife, Mary, explained to me that inside the sarcophagus was a "hunter" whose purpose was, when the right prayers were read, to awake from its sleep and find any unresting souls in the cemetery.

"You see," Mary explained, "there have been disturbances in the cemetery, and people who should have long been at rest are again among us. Your family is worried that your grandparents have been afflicted with this. The hope is that the hunter within this sarcophagus will awake, find the restless soul and bring to an end its undead state, allowing he or she to be laid to rest and the soul to go to the afterlife."

"A vampire?" I asked.

Mary nervously raised her eyebrows in subtle acknowledgement while giving me a half glance, and she said under her breath,

"Wolf's hair." As this was not a woman to shy away from confrontation or to speak her mind, I was left somewhat curious as to why she said this as if she was afraid someone would hear her say it, although before I could question her more, she walked ahead of me toward a stone crypt.

I hadn't noticed that we were approaching the crypt, as I was distracted with the idea that my family had brought this ornate sarcophagus for what I imagined was some archaic ceremony to exorcise a demon or demons from this place. Mildly annoyed at the fact that I hadn't been informed of the intended purpose of our trip, I began to pay less attention to the conversations around me and stared intently at the crypt. It appeared to be roughly the size of a large shed or small garage and made entirely of stone. The front peak of the crypt was topped with a cross, and following a line straight down from the middle of it one could bisect the building into two symmetrical images. At the bottom of this line was the door which we used to enter the crypt.

Allowing my eyes to adjust to the darkness inside, I was left with the impression that daylight was prevented from entering this place, giving it its dark, empty atmosphere. To the left was a small area containing a stone bench for someone to sit on, and to the right was a wall and an old wooden door. My uncle and Thomas carried the sarcophagus in through the door to a small room which housed a square wooden table and a single light. I began to follow them into the room, at which point I was told by Mary to wait outside with my wife, mother, aunt and uncle, and that when the time was right, after the proper prayers had been read, she would call for the rest of us to come in. I looked at the others around me and, this seeming to be the consensus, I agreed and stood by the bench.

Muffled by the wooden door, I could hear some talking from the small room which now housed Thomas, Mary and the sarcophagus. I could only assume that these were the prayers which needed to be read before anyone else could enter the room. I spent this time scouring my memory for a time when anyone in my family had ever spoken of such traditions or practices, and despite my best efforts I could not think of a single conversation when something as spectacularly mysterious as this would have been discussed. The cold and damp air inside the crypt caused my breath to condense as I exhaled, and I watched as it danced in the air in front of my face, slowly billowing up in front of my eyes toward the celling of the crypt in which we now silently stood.

The peaceful silence of my thoughts was suddenly and abruptly disjointed by the violent opening of the wooden door to the little room. The shattering sound of the wooden door crashing into the stone wall reverberated through the crypt, and no doubt outside of it. The initial paralyzing shock of the most violent manner which the door was flung open was quickly broken by the sound of Mary screaming at us from inside the small room.

"Quickly, close the door! In the name of God, don't let it out!"

Mary's voice echoed from behind a plume of dust, which had been raised like a restless soul from its unnatural grave and billowed through the doorway. In a state of paralysis, I watched as my uncle and mother frantically attempted to shut the door. Their efforts seemed in vain as something from the other side of the door, something clearly of great strength, prevented them from closing it. Finally able to break myself from my shocked stasis, I ran to help them. It felt as if we were pushing in futility against the door. Whoever—or, better to say, whatever—was forcing the door open was of such strength that all our efforts proved fruitless and we simultaneously fell back as the door was flung open a second time.

What now stood in the doorway was something that I had never imagined and would gladly never see again. It was the hunter which Mary spoke of. Standing the height of an average man, it failed to fill the door and fully obscure the view of the room behind it. I stared at the creature as it momentarily paused and scanned the room and the people now standing before it.

Its hair was dishevelled and black and hung to its shoulders. Its skin resembled that of a recently deceased corpse whose blood had drained away from the skin, leaving an unremarkable tone of pale grey. Beneath its furrowed eyebrows were the same empty eyes that were engraved into the lid of the wretched sarcophagus that once housed it. Behind them lay no soul. The little bit of unnatural light emanating from the room behind it gleamed off of the creature's fangs, which were now visible as it slowly opened its mouth, stretching its jaw in the same manner as a wolf does as it prepares to move after being disrupted from rest, while staring directly at me.

Looking past the creature, the plume of dust created by its appearance now settled, I could see Thomas lying in a twisted heap on the ground. He lay on his right side with his head twisted in an unnatural manner so that his forehead was pointed down where his chin should be. Thomas's face was covered in his own blood, his eyes still staring and frozen in the final moments of terror which gripped him before his life was taken from him in the most violent of manners. Still from the little room I could hear Mary's cries of horror as she undoubtedly had just watched her husband's murder at the hands of this thing that now approached me with arms outstretched.

The sight of Thomas's mutilated body and the sound of everyone's screams of terror boiled in me a rage which I hadn't felt before and have yet to feel again. The momentary haze of primal anger that filled my body and soul was quickly replaced with the unwelcome feeling of change, a change I had only until that day felt during the brightest full moon. Unaware of how I came to stand eye to eye with this creature, I could now feel its throat firmly in the grip of my right hand. As adrenalin pumped through my body, I could feel my blood rushing though my arm to the tips of my fingers, and as my claws dug into either side of this creature's esophagus, I could clearly hear the tearing of skin and the sound of its throat being crushed under the strength of my hand. I watched as its blood flowed out of its throat and soaked the fur which now covered my hand and arm. I raised the miserable creature up, lifting its feet off the ground. The hunter now swung its arms at my face with hapless futility, attempting to prevent its untimely and unexpected end. The smell of its blood filled my nostrils and was absorbed by every sensory receptor in my nose, signalling a hunger in me which I had been able to suppress with varied success to that day. Acting now from instinct rather than thought, I swatted its pathetic attempts to fight me away, and with my left hand grabbed its disheveled hair, pulling its head back and sinking my teeth into its now exposed and vulnerable neck.

Drinking the blood of this creature, I gnawed at its neck like a rabid wolf until its head was fully separated from its body.

With my hunger now suppressed, I dropped its body and head to the ground, discarding it like common trash.

I slowly turned to look at my family and saw their faces stricken in horror. They were making the sign of the cross repeatedly. I sobered from my blood lust to the realization that none of my loved ones had ever seen me in this wolf-like state. None knew how the taste and desire for blood has had a grip on me so powerful that the mere smell of it lowers me to the instinctive reactions of an animal rather than the rational actions of man.

As I stood there covered in the blood of the creature, staring at my family and them staring at me, I also realized that the intended purpose of this creature I had just killed was not to exorcise demons from the cemetery, but to exorcise a demon brought here. I was that demon, and now those whom I loved and who had brought me to this crypt with the intention of not leaving with me alive stared at me, wondering what I would do with them.

The rage which had just consumed my being was exchanged for an incredibly powerful sorrow and sense of loss that to this very moment—and I can only imagine for all of time—is ingrained in my memory. That day remains so deeply etched in my soulless existence that every day from the moment I wake to the last second before I sleep I remember every detail with painful accuracy, and every sound and smell from that day haunts my every waking moment. Every smell and taste takes me back to that moment when I realized, standing before those whom I cared for most, that I was the creature that was to be destroyed that day, and their intention was to bury me in that stone crypt.

Having found a way to escape the clutches of mortality, I have since that day lost all that was of any value to me in my mortal or immortal life. Now rather than being haunted by the ever-approaching shadow of death, I have been condemned with this curse of immortality, neither able to live among those whom I once longed to be with nor able to end this infernal existence. Haunted with these memories, I curse myself every day. Had I allowed that creature to kill me as was intended by my family, I would be without this pain and they would be able to rest with the knowledge that they had saved my now cursed soul.

Scarlett of Oakwood

Oakwood Cemetery is a place in this town that seems frozen in time. As one of the oldest cemeteries in the area, Oakwood has long run out of space for more burials on its grounds. Standing at the main gate, one can gaze upon the aged and moss-covered tombstones and be forgiven for thinking that they had been transported there from the pages of a Victorian horror story. From this perspective, you would be looking into the grounds of Oakwood facing north, with the stone wall that surrounds the cemetery grounds stretching away from you to the east and west. Connecting the wall at the gate is a wrought-iron archway, and inscribed in the archway is the Latin phrase ABIIT AD MAIORIS: "They have gone to the ancestors." The age of the cemetery is evident by the fact that the main gate is not built to accommodate even a compact car.

Few people visit Oakwood since the direct descendants of those who rest within the cemetery have also long since passed. Most of the names inscribed on the tombstones are unknown to the current residents of the town. The stories of those who are separated from the town by the stone wall have long since been forgotten, although those inside the wall do not suffer the same memory loss. Inside the walls they have returned to their ancestors, although not all remain, nor do they rest peacefully.

With a swift smack from her right hand, Scarlett hit the snooze button on her alarm clock. She lay on her bed awake, staring at the blank emptiness of her white bedroom ceiling. The mechanical buzzing of her alarm clock freed her from the disturbance of a recurring nightmare. Three nights in a row the same dark dream had haunted her sleep, and for three consecutive mornings she lay awake, unrested and pondering its meaning.

Each time the dream started the same way. She is walking an empty cobblestone road, the pathway lit by candle-burning streetlamps. As she walks along this old cobblestone street with its many shops, Scarlett notices how the area is conspicuously void of any activity. Not a soul can be heard; there's not a person in any shop. Each time she wonders why on such a shop-filled street nothing can be seen, nothing can be heard, and nobody else is moving or milling about. No people, no birds, nothing except silence and the flickering movement of light provided by the candlelit lamps lining the street. Shadows jump and move to the movement of the flames, providing Scarlett's eyes with something to focus on other than the sound of sand crunching beneath her feet as she walks.

Coming to the end of the street, she finds herself standing across from an old cemetery, its age evidenced by the faded and crooked headstones facing her. Never does she look left or right to see what else could be in the area. Her attention is seized by the cemetery and its aged and forgotten appearance. Growing in abundance between the headstones are mature willow trees, their branches like long bony fingers hanging from thin drooping arms. The sound of the wind is all there is to fill the emptiness of being alone in this scenery. The wind causes the branches of the willows to sway back and forth, lightly touching the ground like fingers ever so slightly dragging against a tabletop. Scarlett tries to look farther into the cemetery, but all she can see is darkness stretching infinitely behind the willows and headstones.

At this point, Scarlett will hear a hollow noise starting quietly in the distance, almost as a part of the sound of the wind moving the leaves in the trees: the faint sound of a child. As it becomes more distinct, Scarlett recognizes the sound as a child's cry, or screaming. Concerned, she will call out to it, asking if anyone is there, and if they need help. "Are you okay?" she calls into the emptiness of the cemetery. Nothing arrives in response. Taking a few steps, she finds herself suddenly walking through the cemetery. She turns back and the cobblestone street on which she was just standing is now far behind her. She can't understand how, after taking only a few small steps, she finds herself across the street and in the middle of the cemetery. Yet every time she takes those steps, she finds herself far from the street and surrounded by headstones. A sea of pale grey stones protrudes from the ground around her in every direction, stretching into the darkness in crooked lines until they can no longer be seen. Behind her there is the fading light of the cobblestone street, so far in the past that she can only just see its faint glow. It's so far now that Scarlett is only able to recognize the flickering light by the way the shadows jump and dance away into the night.

Scarlett will again hear the scream, only this time closer, more defined and distinct. The sound sends a chill through her body, emanating from her spine and radiating through her until the hairs on her arms and neck coldly stand like the headstones surrounding her. The scream is empty and soulless, a hollow piercing sound which rings in her ears, reverberating in her mind and freezing her in place.

Again she hears it, closer, and the sound washes over her like the tips of a thousand tree branches being dragged across her skin, creating a chill that pulls every hair up and freezes her soul, tensing all her muscles and culminating in a shudder. Despite her efforts to determine the direction of the screaming, Scarlett fails to discern where it is coming from. The echo of the scream still hangs in the air all around her, floating on the wind as it passes through the trees.

Scarlett is startled by a young boy standing in front of her, behind a slanted headstone. He is silently looking at the ground between them. It's as if he has appeared from nothing, silent and emotionless.

"Oh my god! You scared me. I didn't hear you." No response comes from the child, who stares at the ground still.

She nervously regards the boy, no older than eight, motionless. His short black hair does little to cover his face, which in the dim light of the cemetery looks a pale grey.

"Hello? Are you okay? Was that you I heard screaming? Are you alone out here?" she asks. The boy remains motionless.

Scarlett attempts to see anything that may help her determine the boy's identity, and whether it was him screaming, and why. The boy is dressed neatly in a black dress shirt and black pants; he is barely taller than a headstone. Bending down slightly to get a look at his face, Scarlett sees that it is thin and frail with distinctively sharp cheek bones, which suggest he is malnourished, and a skin tone which is pale and clearly hidden from the sun. His dark eyes lie deep in his face, and from them his long, thin nose marks an imperfect line to his mouth. His lips are held tightly together, slightly rolled into his mouth, and he seems to be clamping his teeth on them from the inside.

Scarlett begins to reach forward and takes a half step toward the boy, and he snaps his head up and gazes at her. She freezes in place, staring at the boy, him staring back at her. Doing her best to conceal her fear, she gazes at the blank, emotionless expression seemingly looking right through her.

To Scarlett it seems as if the boy slowly parts his lips, revealing unkempt teeth, and he stretches his mouth beyond what she believes humanly normal. The slow movement is broken as the boy begins to scream and Scarlett can do nothing but cover her ears. The piercing sound of the scream feels like knives piercing her ears. The cold emptiness of the sound reaches into her and she can feel it deep in her mind, deep within her soul. Covering her ears, Scarlett instinctively closes her eyes and steps back from the sound, gripping the sides of her head, but nothing can prevent the sound from piercing deep into her. She opens her eyes slightly to see the boy standing on the tombstone in front of her and reaching out toward Scarlett, his fingers long and bony with jagged little fingernails, dirt-covered and overgrown. His eyes remain empty and lifeless, dark and empty, staring at her with no emotion, no indication of anger, pain or anything that would hint of a human soul behind them. As he opens his mouth she can see his teeth, some missing, others worn away by decay and neglect. He continues to scream and opens his mouth wider, the skin on the sides retracting to allow his jaw to open farther. The sound of bone cracking and snapping causes a feeling of nausea to swell inside Scarlett. She watches as his jaw detaches, almost snapping back so his mouth can continue to open, exposing more decayed teeth. She can only watch as the child's teeth approach.

It is at this point that for the last three nights Scarlett has been spared the remainder of her dream by the mechanical buzzing of her alarm clock. As with the previous two mornings, she just lies there, trying her best to understand why she sees this screaming child each night and why he continues to return to her dreams.

Scarlett and Natasha walked home along the road which framed Oakwood cemetery. Engaged in conversation, the two rarely paid any attention to the activity happening around them. Scarlett was explaining to Natasha the dream which she had been enduring. Fortunately, it had been a few weeks since her last dream of the boy in the cemetery, although she was still shaken by its repetition. Natasha did her best to calm her friend. "Okay Scarlett, let's stop for a coffee and maybe you can focus on something else for a bit."

"Yeah, why not," Scarlett responded.

As the two walked, Scarlett suddenly stopped in front of Oakwood Cemetery. "What's wrong?" asked Natasha.

"Nothing, I just feel like I need to go in here for some reason. Can you come with me?" Scarlett said while looking at the main gate of Oakwood.

"Now?"

"Yes."

"It's getting late. Do you really want to go in there after you just told me about your stupid dream?"

"Yes. I can't explain it, I just need to."

With an exasperated sigh, Natasha agreed to follow her friend into the cemetery.

They walked in among the gravestones, each seemingly more faded than the last. Few names were even remotely legible under the weathering and moss. The farther they walked, the darker it seemed. Scarlett didn't know why she was in here, just that she needed to walk through the gravestones.

"It's kind of eerie, isn't it?" Scarlett asked.

"Yeah, and I don't like it much, so why do don't we get out of here and you can continue your goth fest when the sun is up."

"Shh, just don't worry about it. We'll leave soon," Scarlett said as she grabbed Natasha's arm.

"Listen, I don't know why you needed to come in here, and I don't like you grabbing my arm like that," Natasha said as she pulled away from Scarlett. "But right now I'm leaving." Clearly upset, Natasha pulled away from Scarlett and began walking away through the cemetery.

"Why are you going that way?" Scarlett asked, watching her friend walk into the darkness.

"Because it's the only way I can go. I'm leaving now."

Somewhat annoyed that Natasha was abandoning her in the cemetery, Scarlett snapped back at her, "Fine, whatever, I'll just see you later. I guess we're not going for a coffee."

Natasha didn't respond and Scarlett was left standing in silence.

Scarlett found herself yet again on the empty cobblestone road dimly lit by candle-burning lamps. Looking around, Scarlett noticed that the area was conspicuously void of any activity, which to her seemed particularly odd for a street with so many shops. The only movement that filled the emptiness of the street was the shadows created by the lamps. Each shadow jumped and danced in such a manner that it seemed to spring to life when Scarlett approached it, yet always scurried away from her when she was too close. The mocking movement of the shadows provided Scarlett something to focus her attention on other than the sand crunching beneath her feet as she walked.

As Scarlett approached the end of the cobblestone road, she realized that she was standing across from an old cemetery. She could see the age showing in the faded and crooked headstones which faced the cobblestone street where she stood. Scarlett felt as though she had been here before as she looked at the mature willow trees which seemed to line the pathways between the headstones. The scenery left Scarlett with the impression of a desolate emptiness as she looked farther into the cemetery, seeing nothing but darkness behind the trees, and a heavy silence filled the air, except for the sound of the wind passing through the trees.

Slowly building from the depths of her soul, Scarlett came to the realization that the familiarity she was sensing was more than a bad feeling. Rather, it was the primal instinct within every person—she realized that this was the sense of mortal threat which enveloped her. Like a gazelle on the savannah, she was sensing something that warned her of a danger not yet seen. This danger wasn't unfamiliar and came from a previous experience. *My dreams.* Momentarily frozen in time, Scarlett thought about the environment around her and the sounds and feeling it created. Initially refusing to believe what she was seeing, her acceptance of this reality escaped with her whispered words: "It's happening."

I can't continue. I have to go back, Scarlett thought. *But how can this be real? There must be a reason that I saw it all before.*

Faintly at first, Scarlett heard a noise in the distance, something akin to the sound of a strong wind whistling through an opening in a doorway. As it became more distinct, Scarlett recognized the sound: a child crying or possibly screaming in the distance. Concerned, Scarlett called into the cemetery, "Hello? Are you okay?" She was greeted with silence. Taking a few steps forward, Scarlett found herself standing among the headstones in the cemetery, the flickering lights of the candle-burning lamps on the cobblestone road now in the distance behind her. Looking back, she wondered how after only a few steps she was able to find herself seemingly in in the middle of this old cemetery, surrounded by a sea of pale grey stones protruding out of the ground in all directions.

More distinctly than before, Scarlett heard the screaming again, the hollow sound sending a chill through her body. Closer than before, she heard it again. It washed over her again, scraping her soul like a thousand knives being dragged across her skin, pulling every hair up and freezing her in place. The sound hung in the air, dancing on the breeze and into her mind.

Scarlett turned left and right in a futile attempt to determine the direction the sound was coming from. As she turned, she caught in the corner of her eye a figure standing behind the headstones in front of her. There she stood, a young female dressed all in black, looking down at her feet, her dark straw-like hair only partially covering her face and obscuring her pale skin. Scarlett stared at the girl, appearing roughly the same age and height as Scarlett.

The girl didn't move, she just stared at the ground in front of her.

"I'm so sorry. I didn't see you standing there," Scarlett said. "Are you okay? Was that you screaming?"

With no response, the girl continued to stand motionless, head hanging, staring blankly at the ground.

Scarlett bent down slightly to get a better look at the girl's face and could see her pale greyish skin, sunken cheeks, and dark hollow eyes. "H-hello?" Scarlett said. The girl in the black dress slowly raised her head and stared directly at Scarlett, but her empty gaze made Scarlett feel as though she was staring directly through her. Nothing in the girl's face led Scarlett to believe that the girl knew who she was or that she was there. An emotionless face with empty eyes stared through Scarlett.

The girl slowly raised her arms and reached toward Scarlett, who could now see the girl's hands, bony and neglected. The dirt under her broken fingernails left Scarlett with the impression that the girl had been digging at the ground for some time. Scarlett started to reach back toward the girl, thinking she was looking for help, and the girl began to scream. The hollow piercing sound penetrated Scarlett's soul, and all she could do was cover her ears and close her eyes in an attempt to protect herself from the sound. Before she could open her eyes, Scarlett felt something pulling at her arms. She realized it was the girl pulling her closer to the scream.

The mechanical buzzing of Scarlett's alarm clock again spared from her dream. She lay motionless on her bed, staring at the emptiness of her white ceiling. If only to silence the buzzing of the alarm clock, Scarlett switched it to radio mode and listened to the morning news.

"Police are still looking for any information on the disappearance of Natasha Volkov last week and are urging anyone with information to please contact them as soon as possible. In other news . . ."

A Field of Blackbirds

Morning was signalled by the rising of the early summer sun. A mosaic of colours from bright flowers was woven into the green background of the meadows, accented against the dawn's sunrise. The heat of the early morning sun warmed the field and awakened all life dwelling within it. With the light of the morning, bees began their job of pollination and the insects milled about collecting food. The sound of various insects, winged and crawling, played on the wind like an orchestra. Small mammals poked their heads out from their burrows—the time had arrived for them to scurry about the grass and later return to their homes to feed the young which, still nursing, were not ready to fend for themselves. In the heavens, birds of prey circled, hawks and eagles, each waiting for the burrowing mammals to show themselves in the open.

The awakening of the field's animals was not the only sign of life to break the silence of night. The natural sounds of nature were broken, just as they broke the silence of night, by two gatherings of men. From opposing sides, I heard the growing sound of men waking and preparing for their days, their morning chatter replacing the sounds of the insects. The smell of burning wood preparing final meals clouded the smell of flowers being pollinated in the morning. The sound of men preparing themselves for the coming clash emanated from both ends of the field, ordered chaos gradually replacing the natural sounds which normally filled the air, the sounds of nature giving way to the chorus of war.

It started as a low growling thunder, the first horde of men marching to their position on the field. The thundering sound of a thousand boots on the ground was accompanied by thousands more moving to their positions on the field. Now the first horde was joined by the second, a once foreign horde. The horizon which normally bore treelines and the silhouettes of mountain ranges was gradually replaced by the two groups of men marching to their positions opposite each other. The rolling thunder grew as they approached, the shaking caused by the hooves of their horses sending all the small mammals back to their burrows. Today their young would not eat. The reverberation caused by their drums disturbed the bees—their pollination of the flowers and trees would be forced wait for another day. The birds of prey were soon joined by the scavengers of the skies, creating clouds of hovering wings blackening out the sun. A conspiracy of ravens fluttered erratically above and circled the accumulation taking place on the field below. The presence of the ravens gradually replaced that of the birds of prey, foretelling what was to come.

The playing of zurnas, signalling the approach of the greater swarm of men, danced on the wind and grew with each approaching step. The hollow sound of these woodwind instruments permeated the soul of everyone and everything as they took their positions. They marched to their ghostly music and approached in a such a mass that the wolves and bears in the surrounding woods and mountains fled from the rhythmic thunder created as each boot and hoof hit the ground below. The rumble of the multitude pushed away and replaced the predatory lords that once ruled the forests and mountains. This mass of men by their sheer size crushed all before them under their feet. The small mammals were covered in darkness as the openings of their burrows were closed under the clamour created by their horses, which were adorned with intricate and ornate armour.

The approach of the two bands of men brought with them the sound of steel clanging. The metal they carried—armour, swords and shields—reflected brightly in the sun. The light bouncing from their steel carried the shadow of death with it, cast as the sun rose above the field and the men stood in their places and the reflection from their steel armour and weapons reflected across the field. Silence fell as the men faced their foes. All that could be heard was the crying of the birds above. The ravens with their mocking caws floated far above the soon-to-be-bloodstained field. All the life that normally flourished on this field had been forced into hibernation, holding all life hostage to the calm which pre-empted the bloodletting chaos to follow. The ominous presence of the armies had silenced the wind in the trees, so that even God himself was unable to impose his presence on this fated field. For a moment time had frozen, the life on the field replaced by a darkening silence.

The silence was broken in an instant as one of the men raised his sword above his head and lowered it in the direction of his foes. In this instant, the thunderous sound of a thousand horses galloping and even more men running and bellowing their war cries to the heavens shattered the calm. The ground shook violently under their feet.

The flowers were trampled beneath foot and hoof. What remained of the animals that lived on this field fled for fear of death. Nothing was to be spared from the wrath of these men and nothing will survive their clash on the field. The only undisturbed life was the conspiracy which fluttered and flew above, floating in the heavens, angels of darkness and omens of death waiting for their opportunity when silence again returned.

The shattering sound of steel being forced upon itself permeated the explosion of galloping horses and warring men. It was this sound of clashing weaponry that heralded the first soaking of the dry ground. It was not the first nor the last time that blood stained the soil on this field, but it was this blood on this day that changed the field and the world in which it lived. The once dry ground was gradually, over the course of the day, muddied by the blood of the men who battled on it. The sound of their screams was echoed by the cawing ravens circling above. None below knew that their screams of pain and the percussion of cracking bones danced in the air like a symphonic melody for the black birds hovering in the heavens above. Each spill of blood wet the ground, and the smell of flesh and blood floating in the increasingly warm summer air attracted more of the birds that filled the sky above this field.

As more men flooded the centre of the meadow, all life that made its home there was pushed away. Grass was replaced by blood-soaked mud. Where once small mammals scurried for food, the bodies of men now lay after marching to their death, cut down by the blades of those they called heathen. The bees that once pollinated the flowers and helped them multiply and grow were no longer needed, as the flowers in which they once fed were now nothing more than broken stems, trampled below heavy footfalls. The life that remained flew above the field, hanging over the warring hordes of men, waiting patiently for their time to descend.

Near silence returned to the field, but the roar of thousands of hooves would not be replaced with the buzzing of the bees and other insects or the scurrying of the animals. The life that once existed on the field would not yet return, and all who lived there would wait for some time to meekly return to the shattered field. The two hordes of men had crashed against each other like waves on the rocks of an unforgiving shore, but the current had swept aside as the shore held, forcing the waves to pull back into the sea. The desolation that remained was a panorama of despair: thousands lay dead, others slowly joining those already passed. If not for their laboured moans and the fluttering of the ravens above, there would be nothing but silence on the field. Shields and armoured men covered the once flourishing meadow, and the life that had radiated in the meadow was replaced the pungent scent of death and a silence which could only be welcomed by Kharon, the ferryman of the Netherrealm.

It was not long before the silence was again broken, although it was not the sound of men that disturbed the quieted field. Falling from the heavens, the ravens descended on the field and found their meals among the men who remained. A dark cloud of black-winged demons blanketed the field, and the men who had once dominated the landscape now succumbed to the feeding of the ravens. The cawing was interrupted only by the sound of still warm flesh being torn away. The clash of men and the bloodletting that resulted was the prophesy foretold by their flight above this field.

A maiden of noble house navigated the resulting chaos of bodies, the sound of her steps hidden under the cawing of ravens and cries of dying men. All that once stood with the pride of ill-believed power now lay devastated before her. One by one she visited injured and dying warriors, carrying with her water to sooth their suffering, all nearing a darkness they had thought was meant for their foe. "Have you seen my betrothed?" she would ask, and one by one their voices fell silent beneath a crescendo of conspiracy. Kneeling beside a warrior as noble as she, the word of her love and the fate which he received shattered all hope she had carried.

"The bravery with which he fell will be remembered for all," he said. The warrior described for her the moments of heroism in battle that caused the stain on the field. After recalling all he could, he looked to the west to watch the sun in its final descent. The last moment of warmth he sought was stolen away, because all that could be seen was the blackness of feathers fluttering on the horizon, a dancing orchestral darkness in which he knew he would soon play a part.

That maiden sat beside the dying man in the cold blood-soaked mud, watching as darkness fell. The darkness that enveloped her blanketed me and brought the coolness of the night ahead. Perhaps in the following days or weeks I would be able to slowly return to what I once was. But on this day I was trampled, and my flowers crushed beneath the hooves of horses and feet of men. The life I bore is washed away with the blood of the fallen, and has now become the dinner of the ravens, those dark-winged conspirators that still fly above, now occupying me, the colourful mosaic of flowers replaced with a blackened blanket of feather and talon, their cawing the triumphal song of the victor.

Nikolai and the Butterfly

She perched elegantly, nestled in place, the mirror her pedestal. Slowly the red and black wings of the butterfly opened and closed as if stretching after awakening from a long rest. Nikolai intently watched it sitting on the rear-view mirror of his car. The wings opened and held there for a moment then closed, holding in place yet again. The black lines and swirls in its crimson wings appeared to be two eyes staring back at Nikolai. Open and pause, close and pause, and with each repetition, the movement of the wings, the movement of the eyes staring back, almost demanded that Nikolai's breathing follow their pace. Inhale, hold, exhale hold, inhale, hold, exhale, hold. Nikolai's thoughts drifted from his task at hand and focused on the creature standing and staring on his mirror, mesmerizing his thoughts. His focus was thoroughly concentrated on the swirling, free-flowing, anti-geometric lines that framed and filled the wings of the creature, slowly fluttering, opening with a pause and closing with a pause. So focused had he become on its hypnotic wings that Nikolai failed to notice two things.

The first: he had been sitting in his car alone for the past three hours. Outside it was raining, the heavy drops battering the roof, windscreen and windows. The force of the wind and the rain was enough to keep the birds in their trees, and nocturnal animals that normally roamed the streets remained hidden from the elements. Entombed in the car, Nikolai sat, working through the night and protected from this rain. He was warm and dry, though separated from a source of fresh air. Yet through all this, perching elegantly on its pedestal, sat this crimson and black butterfly. It sat calmly, slowly fluttering its wings, transfixing Nikolai, causing him to remain ignorant of the factors that should have kept this stately crimson creature from finding her place on her pedestal, the mirror, and in Nikolai's mind. The storm that halted all life outside Nikolai's car through the battering of raindrops and gale-force wind somehow did not stop this butterfly from finding its way to its perch on the mirror. This was the first thing that Nikolai failed to notice. He only fixated on her wings, the two black and red eyes hypnotizing his gaze in her direction.

The longer the butterfly sat perched on the mirror, the less aware he was of the world within and out. Slowly a fog began to roll and billow, approaching as time does, ever unnoticed, quietly taking its due from every man, great and weak. Until her dues are paid and there is time no more, does anyone notice that time, like the fog, is always there? The fog slowly billowed and the limit of how far Nikolai was able to see beyond the mirror on his windscreen (not that he even looked past the crimson and black wings fluttering open, pause, closed, pause and again and again, mesmerizing and calm) gradually diminished. In the distance, each streetlight slowly faded away behind a white cloud, but none of this garnered Nikolai's attention; he remained fixated on the butterfly. Its eyes watched as Nikolai became increasingly oblivious to the world around him. The raindrops continued their assault on the windscreen of his car, keeping all manner of life sheltered from it, and the fog, which ought not to have existed, continued to grow in the cab of his car and in his mind, expanding with the flutters of her crimson and black eyes. This was the second thing that Nikolai ought to have noticed.

When the light of dawn broke through the darkness of night, and the clouds of the evening's storm faded away, his colleagues found Nikolai's lifeless body in the driver's seat of the car. He sat where he was when his night started, where he was when he bought a coffee and when the butterfly found its perch on his mirror. Nikolai had been drained of colour; he sat colourless, chalky, grey. His eyes still stared directly at the space between his mirror and the top of the windscreen, no longer resembling those of any person, empty and white, also drained of any colour. All that defined them were two black pinpoints, Nikolai's pupils that once fixated so intently before the colour and life was taken.

What Nikolai's obituary read brought superficial relief to his family and friends. Like so many things surrounding Nikolai's fate, it failed to contain the grim details of his death. Little is said of the fact that the seat in which Nikolai was sitting was soaked, saturated with the blood of a man who died with no apparent wounds, no injury to any major arteries and not a single health problem. The smell of death was entombed in the car, in the seat where he sat, fixated on the crimson and black, the fluttering eyes that stared into him. The red of his blood now stained the grey tone of the seat in which he had been sitting, and that colour left his body a pale grey, barely recognizable as a man. Nowhere was it mentioned that

Nikolai's body was drained. Nobody will discuss that the final sacraments given at his funeral were in vain, because his soul, meant to be saved and ascended to the afterlife, was taken with the colour in his eyes, leaving an empty, soulless gaze. No reports and no discussions, except within these paragraphs, will ever contain the fact that upon opening the door and finding Nikolai's body, his colleagues were greeted by a butterfly with crimson and black wings fluttering out through the opened door, taking with her all that was now missing. These are the circumstances surrounding the death of Nikolai and the butterfly.

In the Darkness

Demos felt a sharp jab to his ribs as the haze of deep sleep dissipated. His eyelids felt as if they were weighted down by stones, but he forced them open in an attempt to gaze through the blur that distorted his view of the source of the jabbing. *Why is she bothering me already?* he thought, believing the source of the problem to be his wife. *What in hell could possibly be so important that she needs to wake me up like that?* All too often he failed to get the rest that he needed from her desire to start the day early. Although he had no choice but to concede the fact, at least to himself, that the nocturnal lifestyle he led probably didn't help his situation. He felt this as he was abruptly woken from a deep sleep in which he had not gotten the rest that he needed.

At forty-three years old, Demos still strived to live the fast life of a man in his early twenties. Late nights and bottomless drinks were habits he learned in university and was intent on keeping. While in university, Demos studied international commerce and excelled at his chosen course of study. In those years he realized that he needed drinks, women and money to excel and succeed. The drinks and the women were things he made a conscious effort to conquer every weekend, and the completion of his degree would help ensure the third was conquered in due time.

This was a partial contributing factor to Demos's slightly aged appearance. Rather than a man in his early forties, Demos appeared to be closer to his early fifties, though he believed the general style and manner in which he carried himself could make up for the unfortunate consequence of expedited aging. Demos's personal sense of style is something he prized greatly; for him it is not enough to dress in a suit, it must be designer, and on that point, what is the sense in wearing the best and most expensive brands if people don't know? From the moment he could discern what style was, Demos ensured he followed his chosen path of image.

He began to stir, but before his vision could clear he received another sharp jabbing pain to his ribs. "Oh, for fuck's sake!"

This time Demos sat up quickly, prepared to give his wife hell for waking him in such an annoying and unpleasant way. He knew they had no early plans, and it wasn't Sunday so she couldn't be having one of her "religious" moments, where suddenly everyone has been a bad Christian and we all have to go and confess our sins to some old guy in a robe, and then afterwards we can all go out for lunch and he can pretend to be Charlie Churchgoer and display to the world the perfect pious family that we have. Oh, fucking joy. But not this time. No way in hell was he going to be playing that role today. It's not Sunday and we don't have plans, so there is no reason to be such a pain in the ass. *This is it. This is the day. She's gonna hear what I have to say about this and her fickle desires for a better life.* As the thoughts continued to run through his mind, his anger grew exponentially. *Good, bad or indifferent it's not going to make a—*

"Wake up. This is neither the time nor the place for you to be sleeping."

Before he could utter a word, he came to the sudden realization that it wasn't his wife's voice that was interrupting his sleep. It was a man's voice, an older man at that. The weathered and tired sound to the voice was somewhat familiar. On second thought, even the way this unknown person uttered the words *wake up* sounded as if this was not the first time he had said them. Demos now thought the man must have been there for a while, trying unsuccessfully to wake him up. The tired annoyance in his voice left Demos with the impression that this seemingly elderly man had been at this for a while, and now Demos was finally responding to him. As his vision began to clear, he was able to see that he wasn't in his bedroom; in fact, there was nothing familiar about where he was at all. His head darted left and right, and the fog of his sleep began to dissipate. He now knew he wasn't on a bed of any kind; he was lying on the ground outside somewhere. The anger that had overtaken him initially gave way to confusion and some embarrassment. *Great, now she'll have ammo when she tells me to quit drinking,* he thought. *It must have been a hell of a night, but I can't remember the last time I passed out in public. Shit, this could be bad. I can just imagine the "you have to slow down and lead a healthier life" speech that I'm going to get now. Well, the hell with it, I might as well find my car.*

Demos sat up to the sight of a man whose face appeared to have been weathered by rigours that only time can exact.

The figure standing in front of Demos was an elderly man of average height. His general appearance left Demos with the impression that his decline into the winter of his life was not defined by a comfortable pension and the Freedom 55 stage, but resembled a war of attrition which, by his appearance, he was slowly losing. He wasn't a hideous man who would be better kept away from public view, but he gave the appearance of being weathered and tired. The man did not look directly at Demos, but Demos could see the man's eyes. He appeared to be staring at something in the extreme distance, but with no focal point. Demos thought that his gaze was cold, empty and emotionless. His hair appeared as though it had been allowed to grow to a length well beyond that which you would expect for a man of his age. Demos could not tell for sure from his vantage point, but it appeared that the man's hair was well past his shoulders, with a colour that would be expected from someone who had lived the years that he appeared to have lived. His hair was mostly grey with streaks of black, and it draped his head in a way that would make one believe they were staring through prison bars upon a cloudy and uninspiring landscape. Demos thought that the few fleeting streaks of black hair scattered upon his head looked like the final few enclaves of his long-passed youth fighting their eventual capitulation.

Regardless of his disheveled appearance, it was clear to Demos that the elderly man was standing over him with some purpose.

"Do you need money?" Demos asked.

"Don't be ridiculous. All I need from you is for you to get up. You can't stay here for all of eternity," he replied.

"Thanks for the newsflash, gramps. I have no intention of staying here. In fact, now that you've taken it upon yourself to wake me, I'll be on my way home," Demos snapped back in an annoyed and sarcastic tone.

"You're too young, too young, Demos, too young," the man stated as he turned and began to shuffle away.

"Hey! How the hell do you know my—" Demos stopped mid-sentence as he took in the scenery around him.

In all actuality one would describe what Demos saw less as scenery and more as *desolation*, particularly when one took into account Demos's reaction to the landscape before him. He stood frozen in a confused state of shock at what he saw. The sky was a particularly sombre collection of grey tones. There didn't even appear to be a place for sunlight to shine, if there even was a sun to shine at all. Demos thought that despite the greyness of the sky above him, the landscape that surrounded him was far more devastating to his consciousness. Ahead of him in the direction where the annoyed elderly man was slowly shuffling away, Demos observed a long, straight roadway or path. It extended a distance far enough that its final destination was unobservable. The roadway was flanked by wooded areas on both sides, although the trees appeared to have been devastated by some type of natural disaster or even warfare. Many of the taller trees had their upper halves torn away or snapped off, leaving stumps that extended twenty feet in the air and were capped with jagged edges jutting to the skyline, reminiscent of the tops of a palisade from medieval Europe. Although, intermittently dispersed amongst the ominous jagged treeline were fallen trees, most with their roots attached. Demos noticed that the sheer size of the trees was enough to emphasize their ancient age. And despite the size and age of the fallen trees, they had somehow been ripped out of the ground, leaving their roots above ground and unable to provide them with the nourishment needed to keep them alive. As such, these fallen giants lay dying and dead, rotting away into the ground that once sustained them. As for the trees that remained standing and undamaged, they provided little accent to the dull sky in the background. The trees that had any leaves appeared as if the colour in them had slowly been drained away.

Adding to the unearthly atmosphere was the fact that Demos didn't observe any animals, anywhere. Even in the most densely populated urban centres there are some types of animals milling about—squirrels, pigeons and so on. There wasn't even the sound of animals in the distance; all that Demos could hear was the sound of sand crunching beneath the feet of the elderly man as he slowly shuffled away.

"Why am I too young?" Demos asked in a manner that emphasized the fact that he didn't expect a response. He remained frozen as the elderly man walked away. Demos knew he wasn't at home, although he still didn't know where he was. The unearthly appearance of the scenery around him only solidified his confusion. He had just spent the last few minutes talking to some unknown elderly man about nothing, and had learned nothing of where he was and how he got there. Surveying his situation, Demos decided that his best course of action was to follow the elderly man, although he also felt he had no other option. His mind raced as he followed the dishevelled figure along the dirt path.

I need to figure out where I am, he thought. *Unfortunately, this old bastard doesn't seem too interested in talking to me to give me much in terms of some idea of what the hell is going on. He was hellbent on getting me up and moving, but it'd be nice if he actually gave me some idea of where I'm supposed to be moving to. I mean, for fuck's sake, who wakes someone up, tells them to get moving then just fucking walks away? What's worse is he's being a miserable old bastard about it. And now, to make the situation worse, I'm following him trying to figure out where to go. How fucking insane is that? I don't know where I'm going, where I am and who this old bastard is. Jesus fucking Christ, can you give me a hand here?*

"Hello?" Demos yelled to the elderly man. "Hello? Can you give me some idea of where we are? I mean, you wake me up from a dead sleep in some mad rush to get me up and moving, but you don't tell me where I am, and you don't tell me where I'm supposed to be going. You just shuffle off like a disgruntled goat."

"Demos," the elderly man said as he continued to shuffle his way down the path, "he won't be helping you anymore. You are where you are supposed to be, and I'm the furthest thing from a goat. You have no obligation to follow me, nor do you have any obligation to accept anything I am telling you. What you do have to understand is that you are in a place where you will not be able to return from. You have made many decisions in your life that led you here. Much like everyone else who has come here before you."

"Here? Where exactly is here? You haven't answered any of my questions with anything more than thinly veiled riddles. And you don't even have the decency to stop and look at me while you're talking to me. So no, I don't understand where I am, and I don't see how I can accept what you are telling me when you're clearly not telling me anything." Demos stopped and threw his hands in the air in frustration, then let them drop on his head. He held them on opposite sides of his head and looked up exasperated and confused. "Why don't you give me a simple answer? Start with this: where exactly am I?" Demos yelled into the air.

The elderly man stopped and, still facing away from Demos, began to speak.

"Demos, where you are now is a place that theologians and philosophers have discussed throughout the ages, and will continue to discuss long into the future. This is, all at the same time, a place of great joy and happiness and a place of despair. Whether you experience joy or despair is purely dependant on you and your actions leading to this time."

"Another riddle. Thanks. Thanks for nothing. Your inability to give me a straight answer only leads me to believe that you have no idea where we are, and you're probably—and I only judge this from your ragged appearance—intoxicated. How is the box you live in this time of year? I would assume the cold wind I'm feeling blows right through it. I mean the insulation can't be very good, is it? But really, how would you know the difference? Years of crack and booze have probably rendered you numb to any feeling of the world around you. I'm impressed that you've been able to carry on a conversation with me this long without defecating on yourself. Congratulations."

"Demos, it's this type of anger and disrespect that seems so ingrained in you that has led you to where you are. I was hoping that you would be able to figure out where you are yourself and what your situation is, as this is the natural way of things. But unfortunately, you're proving yourself to be as unsavoury a character as you're billed to be."

"What the hell does that mean? And how do you know my name?" Demos responded.

The elderly man stopped walking and turned to face Demos. He stared with a look in his eyes that placated Demos's anger and replaced it with a type of nervousness that he could not understand. The elderly man's gaze was not one of anger, and it seemed to be void of any recognizable emotion that Demos could understand. "Demos, you don't know where you are because you are somewhere where you have never been before. Your earthly life has ended, and you have transcended from it to something that you would understand as an afterlife."

"Are you saying I'm dead? If you're threatening me, you've got another thing coming," Demos responded, but the tone of his voice betrayed him. It would have been clear to anyone listening that his response to the elderly man was not one of aggression or strength. His voice carried the fragility of shock and fear, despite the intended strength of his words. Demos's thoughts began to race through his mind. *What is he trying to tell me? He can't be serious; none of this makes any sense. I need to figure out what exactly is going on. I can't be dead, this isn't heaven, none of this fits, nothing makes any sense.* Demos's confusion began to compound to the point where he couldn't even focus on where he was. A feeling of emptiness enveloped him, and as he looked around at the landscape surrounding him his vision began to blur. His eyes darted from left to right as he attempted to gain a level of understanding and clarity on his current situation, but nothing seemed to help him. As his confusion exponentially grew, his consciousness diminished at the same rate. His blurred vision faded to darkness, and although he attempted to speak his words seemed as if they were lost in his mind.

Demos's consciousness seemed to be re-establishing itself, although he still didn't seem to know where he was. Still enveloped in darkness, his thoughts did little to assure him of where he was or what was going on. This is what he did know: he had woken up in a strange park or something; there was an old, disheveled man, who for some reason knew his name, telling him that he was dead; and the world around him looked as if he had been transported to some distant battlefield, in both time and geography. Other than this there was nothing else to know.

"Wait!" he yelled to the elderly man. "Just wait. How can I possibly be dead? I'm only forty-three, and I'm not even sick. What you're telling me doesn't make any sense. On top of that, if I'm dead, where are St. Peter and the gates of Heaven?"

The elderly man spoke. "You watch too many movies. What you understand to happen after your life ends has little to do with what is really happening to you now. Where you are now is both heaven and hell, light and dark. All that you've done in life has led you here."

Demos laughed to himself and then spoke. "So my wife was right? No church, no heaven?"

"No. Your life has led you here. You don't listen to what I say, and you've allowed that arrogance to dictate your life to this point. I've told you: this is what you understand as the afterlife, this is both heaven and hell, or whatever anybody wants to call it. Tell me, Demos, what do you see around yourself?" Knowing the answer to his question, the elderly man turned and attentively waited Demos's response.

"Nothing. Dead trees, a dirt path, and an old man who has seen better days."

"Exactly. Nothing, dead trees, a dirt path, and at this point your only source of information, which you choose to ignore and insult. Yet you don't allow what you see to speak to you and help you understand your situation. Stop and think for a minute, even a second. Take in what I've told you of where you are and what you see. From there, understand your interpretation of theology. You believe the afterlife is divided into heaven for the good and hell for the wicked. I've told you that heaven and hell, as you understand it, are both here where you and I are standing. This is it. Nothing more, no pearl gates, no rivers of fire, nothing more, nothing less, depending, of course, on how you arrived where you are now."

"Listen, gramps," Demos snapped back, becoming increasingly annoyed at the fact that the elderly man refused to answer his questions the way he believed they should be answered. "If I'm dead and this is heaven, then why is it so dark, so depressing, so goddamned desolate? You can't tell me the afterlife is here, when nothing I recognize is before me."

"You will recognize it when the time comes." With that, the elderly man turned away from Demos and walked down the path.

For a minute Demos stood still in the middle of the path, attempting to digest what he had been told. He still refused to accept that he was no longer alive, but he couldn't find anything to refute what he had been told. The elderly man, whom he obviously doesn't know, knows him, knows his personality. And wherever he is right now is completely unfamiliar to him. It is unworldly. There is nothing around, just the piercing sound of nothing and nowhere.

A sudden panic paralyzed Demos as the thought that he was no more sunk in. "I'm not Demos? I'm dead. No, it can't be . . . how could I no longer be if I am? I'm here but I'm not someone anymore. Fuck, no, it can't be!" Numbness overtook his senses and paralysis gave way to pain, deep inner pain that he had never experienced before. This wasn't physical pain, it was something that enveloped him, permeating his soul and becoming a part of his being, and as he felt it he realized he simply wasn't anymore.

Demos wanted to cry, run and scream all at the same time, yet all he could do was stand frozen in empty pain, empty feeling, at the realization that no longer would he return home, see his wife and children, never again experience the joy of daily experience. This was over, to be replaced with this monochromatic world in which he stood now. Demos tried to move to look at what was around him but all he could manage was to dart his eyes left and right. This only served to send him into a deeper panic, and everything he tried to look at became random blurs washed into the grey background.

Slowly Demos began to calm down. The panic dissipated, and he was left feeling—nothing. Demos realized he was lying in the path now, staring at the grey sky which wasn't clear nor cloudy, just grey. With his wits somewhat about him, Demos sat up and looked around. He still saw the grey-toned sky accented with felled and falling trees. Silence was all he could hear. No longer was the elderly man walking down the path. The crunching of sand beneath his feet was replaced with nothing, empty nothing. But as Demos looked to the line of trees bordering the path on either side, he saw what looked like people sitting hunched amongst the treeline like so many rocks that had been displaced on the side of a highway by vehicles speeding by.

"Hello!" Demos yelled.

Neither response from the huddled people nor echo greeted his words, just empty silence.

"Hello? Can you hear me?"

Still nothing. The people in the treeline didn't flinch or speak. They just sat huddled amongst the trees, still and silent.

Demos stood up and began to walk toward them. The crunch of sand returned to his ears, breaking the silence thaat otherwise overwhelmed his senses. Demos walked what felt like a mile to the first person he saw. *What are they doing?* As he approached the first person, he realized it was a woman who was huddled low to the ground and close to the tree. Curled up as she was, with her arms hugging her knees, it was impossible to tell how old or tall she was. She just sat there with her forehead resting on her knees, unmoving.

As Demos reached her, he placed his right hand on her left shoulder and said, "Hey, are you okay?"

Slowly the woman raised her head to look up at Demos, who was now standing bent over with his head slightly above and in front of hers. Her long dark hair first covered then fell to the side of her pale face. The woman looked directly at Demos, and as she did he felt overtaken by a cold that enveloped his entire body. By looking at her, Demos could tell she had once been an attractive woman, but her once vibrant face had now been replaced with one of desolate emptiness. Her skin was pale white and her light eyes were framed by darkness, not like you would expect from someone lacking rest but far darker, a black ring contrasting the colourless white of her skin. Her lips were thin and pale grey with what Demos though was a hint of blue. As the woman looked up at Demos, it appeared as though she didn't see him standing there and her gaze was penetrating him. She stared up as if looking into eternity. He stood frozen, staring back at her and waiting for her to speak, but she didn't, nor did her eyes move. They remained frozen, her pupils dilated into pinpoints, which faded gradually into the whites of her eyes with almost no distinction, directly in the middle of her open, empty gaze. She didn't squint; rather, her eyes were wide open as if they were attempting to take in whatever little amount of light they could. She stared into nothing, her face completely devoid of any emotion or thought.

"Can you hear me?" Demos said again. "How long have you been sitting there? I didn't even see you when I was walking with the old guy. Did you see me?"

Without the slightest change in her expression, the woman slowly lowered her head and her dark straw-like hair cascaded down over the sides of her face and covered her empty gaze until her forehead again rested where it had come from.

Demos stood up straight. The woman remained still as a stone, resting on the tree, which supported her weight. As he looked to her right shoulder where it touched the tree, Demos wondered how long she had been huddled here in this position, unmoving and silent. Would the tree grow over her and eventually make her a part of its trunk and root system? Demos raised his eyes away from the motionless woman and looked into the forest, which now seemed to expand infinitely in all directions around him. He realized that at the base of nearly every tree was not a stone, but another person huddled into a ball on the ground sitting motionless, hugging their legs with their heads on their knees. They blended into their surroundings as if they were painted onto them, intended to be camouflaged from the casual gaze and only noticeable if one was to stare into this forest and examine every tree individually.

Demos wondered what all this was, why all these people were huddled against the trees. He stepped away from the woman and walked to a man huddled into another tree to his left. This man was huddled in the same position as the woman. Every other person in the forest, for that matter, wasn't only leaning against a tree but nestled between two roots which spread from the bases in a V shape, and eventually into the ground below. The roots appeared to hold the unknown man in his place, practically hugging him into the tree's trunk. Demos stood before this man and stared for a minute again, wondering what caused him to be in this position and how long he had been here. He didn't dare speak to him, nor did the thought of touching him as he had with the woman cross his mind. He didn't want to see what the man looked like, or the same empty gaze he had seen in the woman's eyes. Demos stood motionless for minutes, staring at the man, before he finally came to and realized he couldn't just stand here aimlessly. He walked back to the path.

At this point he decided that he would follow the elderly man, if for no other reason than it seemed as if he had somewhere to go, and maybe he could find someone to explain to him what he was to do now.

Demos felt that he had been walking for what seemed like days and hadn't reached anything, nor had he seen anyone except the people huddled into the trees. Still none looked up, moved or made a sound. He wondered if walking down this path was to prove fruitless and if he should just find himself a tree to huddle into. But still he pressed on, walking to an unknown destination away from nothing he could discern or describe.

Demos looked down at himself and noticed that the fibres of his once well-manicured suit and shoes had become clogged with the dust from the path. The black of his clothing was slowly being overtaken by the dull grey of dust and dirt. *Grey,* he thought, *great.* As he walked, Demos saw the silhouette of a person walking toward him. "Hello!" he called out. "Um, can you hear me?"

"Hello!"

The silhouette called back! It sounded like a man's voice, or it could be a woman with a deeper voice—who cares, Demos thought. *It's someone I can talk to! Finally, good fucking god, finally!* he exclaimed in his mind. Demos picked up the pace a bit to reach this person. Although he felt as if his feet lagged behind him somewhat, he didn't feel tired, but for some reason his legs just didn't move with the same enthusiasm as he felt in his mind. It didn't matter; he had walked this far and he was determined to reach this person, if for no other reason than to talk to someone. *Someone who can and will respond!*

As Demos reached the person, he could see it was a man. At first look the man appeared to be in a somewhat more disheveled state than Demos, but did not have nearly as weathered a look as the elderly man. He appeared to be of slightly above-average height, with scraggily grey and brown hair that reached roughly to his cheekbones, which themselves were protruding from the sides of his somewhat concave face. He appeared to be decently dressed, although his clothes were certainly weathered from being worn for far too long. He wore a white dress shirt which was stained from dirt and dust—more than likely the same dust which was now attaching itself to Demos's clothing, and his jeans were torn at the bottom from being worn and stepped on for far too long. Regardless of his appearance, Demos needed to speak with this man. Maybe he could provide some answers. "Hey, um . . . hi."

"Ah, hi," the man responded.

"I'm Demos. What's your name?"

"Um, it's, ah . . . I can't remember." The man responded with a confused and lost look on his face. He stared passed Demos and looked around in bewilderment of his surroundings.

"Okay, well, I'm completely fucking lost. Do you have any idea where we are?" Demos blurted out, ignoring the fact that this man didn't even know his own name. But that didn't matter at this point; Demos was becoming desperate and needed to speak to someone, anyone.

"Well, um—we're, well, still on the path, that's for sure. Oth-other than that, well, we're not with the happy people."

"Happy people? There are more people here? Where are they?" Demos felt a slight glimmering of hope at the prospect that there may be more people around, people that could talk and respond to him, and if they're happy there might be a chance they've figured this place out!

"They're . . . that way." The man pointed back in the direction from which he had come. "You know, I kind of gave up on staying with them. They just don't see things the way I do, you know."

"What do you mean they don't see things the way you do? They disagree with you?" Demos asked, worried about the answer that the man was going to give.

"Well, when you look over there"—the man pointed to Demos's right, to the forest where the people huddled into the trees—"tell me what you see."

"In the forest? Well, it's a dark wood with a lot of dead trees, and—" Demos stopped before saying anything about the people huddled into the trees.

"People huddled into the roots of the trees? Yeah, that's what I see too. But the people back there see a healthy forest and stones, and grass and all sorts of stuff that's not there. You see it or you don't." The man seemed to become increasingly agitated as he spoke. "So you see what I see. You're not like them. You're like me."

Demos stared at the man, confused at the apparent fragility of his current state of mind. *He must have always been like this, and regardless, these other people must know something that he and I don't,* Demos thought.

"Where are they? We need to go there and find out how they see what they see," Demos said to the man.

"What? Go back to that? Not a chance. I'm getting as far away from them as possible. Never going back, never, it won't happen. You're new here, I can see it. You will see it too. You can't go to them. No, go. Go and see them."

With that, the man started walking past Demos. Demos watched him walk away, perplexed at his demeanor, although now thoughts slowly seeped into Demos's mind about the possibility of becoming like this man. *I'm not going to become like him, no, he must have been a little unstable when he died anyway. Plus, come on, who doesn't like being around happy people? That's the whole reason I was always out drinking—happy drunks, happy singing drunks.*

Demos had now confirmed in his mind that the best course of action was to continue his journey in the direction in which the man said the happy people were. This could not be any more certain: if he could find the happy people, he could find out how they see things better than he does. This was his chance. If he was going to be here for all eternity, he sure as hell wasn't going to be miserable and surrounded by people huddled into trees. Now was the time for decisive action.

Good god, does this path just continue on forever? Demos thought, becoming somewhat frustrated at the fact that he hadn't found the happy people. Demos looked around and realized that the farther he walked along the path, the darker the horizon ahead of him became. He felt as if he was slowly walking toward the centre of a black hole that greedily devours all light that casually enters its gravitational pull. Looking behind him, Demos did not see any reprieve from the lack of light that he was surrounded by. He continued forward toward the darkened horizon with little more than a fleeting hope that he might find some of the happy people.

Demos's legs became heavier and moved slower as he did all he could to will them forward. Again he thought to himself that he wasn't physically tired, but his legs and arms felt weighed down and his feet dragged on the sandy path. The crunching of sand under his feet was all Demos could hear again. It shattered the ominous silence surrounding him. Finally, Demos stopped walking. He felt as if he couldn't go another step. He stared aimlessly in front of him, not seeing anything and not looking at any specific point. After a few seconds of staring at nothing, Demos closed his eyes and slowly dropped to his knees. He stayed there, in the path, on his knees, for an unknown amount of time. With his eyes closed, Demos didn't even dare think. The surroundings were silent and his mind was equally empty and quiet.

After some time, Demos heard it again, the crunching. Initially he didn't think anything of it, assuming it came from underneath his own feet, but as soon as thought entered his mind, Demos realized it couldn't be him, as he was on his knees and motionless. Demos opened his eyes apprehensively at first, not wanting to allow his hopes to rise. As his vision cleared, he saw two silhouettes walking toward him. As the two figures came closer, he could see that it was two people, a man and a woman, talking jovially. Neither person seemed to notice him kneeling in the pathway until he spoke.

"Hello?"

"Oh, hello," said the man. "We didn't notice you there."

"I figured. Where are you coming from?"

"Oh, nowhere really. We were relaxing in the light with some people back that way." The man pointed in the direction that Demos had been walking. "But then we decided to go for a walk and see the trees in bloom here in the forest."

"Bloom? Where do you see bloom? Never mind, how is it you see that? I can't see flowering trees anywhere."

The man looked at Demos, perplexed. "We just do. It's everywhere. It's what we see. You should come with us. We will show you the beauty of this forest."

"No, I-I think I'll just continue to where you came from . . . there're more people there, aren't there?"

"Of course," exclaimed the woman. "It's fantastic over there; go tell them you came from the forest—some of them will be so jealous. You see, a lot of the people down by the light, they don't really explore. They're happy where they are, and they don't see a need to. But why not explore when there is so much to see here!"

"Uh, yeah, I suppose. Well, maybe I'll get going now."

"Enjoy your walk," the woman responded as she and the man began walking away. "There's some beautiful stones lining the pathway!"

Yeah, stones, Demos thought. *They're not fucking stones, they're people.* Demos slowly got up to his feet, first resting his right hand on his knee to support his weight and finally standing straight up. His single fleeting moment of hope felt as if it had been stepped on by the overly cheerful and annoying demeanor of the two people he just encountered. He found that he wasn't really angry about his encounter with the cheerful people; he felt as if his spirit had been weighted down under the realization that the disheveled man he met earlier on the path may have been right in his assessment of Demos's situation.

I just don't understand how they could see something that isn't there. My god, I mean, it's either a dead forest or not. It can't both! This is ridiculous. And what light are they talking about? They point to the darkness and tell me it's light. They must be insane! This is why I never did hard drugs. Demos laughed to himself. *Flowers! Beautiful flowers and stones!* He continued to laugh. *Oh my goodness, where could they have come from that they saw light in darkness and flowers amongst dead trees! What I should have done was told them off. I can imagine how that conversation would have went.*

Demos stopped in the path and looked to his left. "Hey, mister and miss happy-go-lucky! Why don't you go to hell!"

He jumped in place and looked to his right. "Thanks, man! I love you too! You're so very kind, can I give you this flower?"

He again jumped in place and turned his head to the left. "For sure, thanks for the dead branch, you stupid fuck. Look at you, you can't even see what's there!"

Jumping in place again, Demos collapsed to the ground, laughing hysterically. Gradually his laughter turned to silence, and he stared blankly at the grey sky above with its lack of brightness and definition. He scanned to the left and right, slowly examining the treetops and the damaged and dying trees that flanked him. "They can't see it, right?" The fragility in his voice surrendered any notion that he was sure of what he was seeing or of what he even believed anymore. Doubts of what he saw and felt began to flood his mind as lay in the silent, empty path. No more did he hear the crunching of feet nor was there anyone to question what he saw. Two things remained sure in his mind: the happy couple came from the same direction as the disheveled man, and he was going to this place, wherever and whatever it was.

Demos raised himself to a sitting position and looked down at himself. When he was woken by the elderly man he was dressed well in a clean suit and dress shoes, tie and all. Now what he saw was nothing more than an empty shadow of his earliest memory of this place. His suit jacket and tie had long ago been discarded; his shirt was now missing buttons and resembled less a dress shirt worn in the corporate boardrooms of the world and more a dirty rag whose encounter with a washing machine was long overdue. The sight of his dress pants only further damaged his spirit, with their once-tailored cuffs now replaced with loose strings and tears. His shoes, while still intact, were no longer black, and those damn loose strings made them look even worse. *Wasn't the dirt enough?* he thought.

He stood up, looked into the distance, into the encroaching darkness, took a deep breath and spoke to himself. "All right, we can do this. There's no reason we can't go there, find out what's going on and what these people are all talking about." He knew by the manner in which the words came from his mouth that he wasn't approaching this place with a sense of determination; it had been replaced by a sense of desperation. He needed an answer. He needed people who could help him. Nothing that he saw or heard made sense. He took one step toward the darkened horizon, then a second, and slowly he moved in the direction where, he believed, his future lay waiting.

As he walked, the darkness seemed to slowly filter around him and the grey tones of the world he had woken up in seemed to be replaced by a cold darkness. The trees with their huddled people remained, although now he could not look farther into the forest. He knew it stretched to what seemed to be infinity, but he could no longer see the distance that he had earlier. As he shuffled his way down the path, he saw all kinds of people milling about. Some looked confused and bewildered at their surroundings, while others seemed to admire the forest and its contents. There was a man who walked the path in the same direction, although slower, who seemed to suffer from kyphosis—his back was hunched and his hands could have dragged on the ground as he walked. Slowly the kyphotic man staggered his way to the treeline. Demos shook his head as he looked down to notice that, along with his altered gait, he had begun to slump his shoulders slightly forward.

Then there was a group of women ahead to his left who laughed and huddled around the edge of the path speaking about flowers. He laboriously lifted his head and strained to look at what they had found. Dead leaves—they were smelling and laughing about dead foliage. This infuriated him. *Why do they smell that?* he thought. He rubbed his eyes and continued to shuffle down the pathway, although now he seemed to drift from side to side as he walked. The farther he travelled, the less he could see of the people who were milling about. Many were but silhouettes in his line of sight, others were now blurs in his peripheral vision. When he turned his head to look, he saw only trees and darkness. The people must have walked away before he turned to look at them, he thought.

None of this mattered. All that was important was for him to continue walking, and then find someone who could help him see the light that the couple talked about. It couldn't be far now, and everything would soon be as it should. As he looked around, he could see more people milling about. They all seemed to be engaged in some type of activity, but all this took place under a vale of silence. Again the only sound that he could hear was the crunching of sand under each step. In fact, by this time his steps had been replaced with the sound of his feet dragging underneath him, and the crunching of each step was elongated into a scrape. Gradually, all he heard was the dragging of his feet and the scraping of sand as the soles of his shoes forcibly removed the granules of sand under him.

Soon he could no longer feel the movement of his feet under him nor was there the sound of sand scraping beneath his feet. Silence remained and darkness enveloped the path. *I must be close now,* he thought. The light that the others saw was the darkness that he approached, and as it was all around him he couldn't be far now. Or possibly he was where he was travelling to, and all that he needed to do now was clear his vision, see through the darkness and he would know where he was.

As if to shatter the silence, he heard it again, the crunching of sand underneath feet. Someone was around, he could hear the walking—not heavy like his own feet on the sand. They were more direct and deliberate. These weren't the steps of the elderly man, either. Still the darkness around him wouldn't clear to allow him to see anything.

He felt a hand on his left shoulder. With the sensation of a touch, it seemed as if his entire nervous system had been awakened. He could feel that he was sitting with his feet close to him and his arms wrapped around his shins. His head was as heavy as a boulder, and it took all of the strength in the muscles of his neck to raise his forehead from where it rested on his knees. Slowly, he raised his head until he looked up to the silhouette of someone standing above him.

As the fog in his eyes cleared and the contrast of this person's shadow against the relative brightness behind them cleared, he could see a woman standing over him. She bore a resemblance to someone he knew, but he couldn't clear his mind enough to recognize her. She was speaking, but he couldn't make out any of the words. Eventually, the silence was broken.

"What's your name?" she asked.

And with the sound of her voice a flood of memories crashed into his mind as he stared up at her. Unable to speak, his eyes slowly scanned the scenery around them. He was huddled on the ground, leaning into the trunk of a tree. The roots had grown around him and were holding him in place. The woman standing above him was his wife, but all she could see was that he was a person huddled into a tree. He did what he could to force words out of his mouth but nothing came; not a sound was made. He knew now that if she could see him the fate that he endured would be waiting for her, and all the pain his soul experienced on its descent to this place where he now sat huddled and alone was amplified to an unimaginable level. He knew what waited for her, but she did not. All he could do was blankly stare into her eyes, filled with the innocence of not knowing what was to come. Defeated and unable to muster even the slightest motion or sound to indicate that he knew her, he closed his eyes and lowered his head until it rested on his knees and the silent darkness returned.

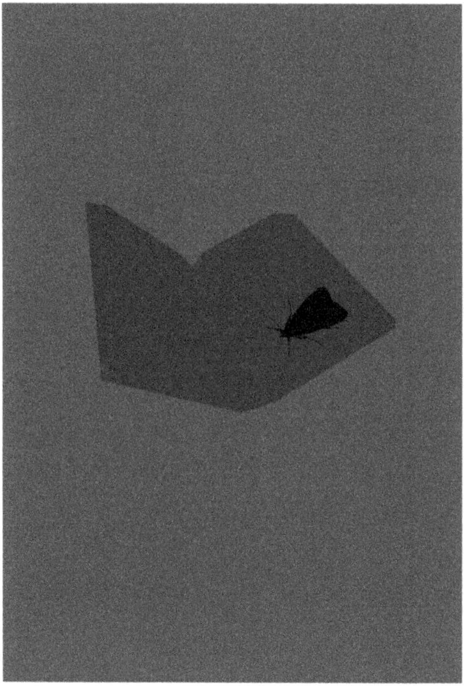

The Little White Moth

Tonight, Ana sat at John's bedside while he slowly ate his soup. At this late stage of the cancer, his appetite was only a fraction of what it had once been. Despite that, he smiled at her while eating. "It's pretty good, you know, for hospital food. Did you know, it's a well-known fact that hospital food is as bad as it is because even disease and sickness can't stand the bland taste. It's actually a tactic developed by the ancient Chinese to heal people through deliberately bad culinary practices."

Both Ana and John laughed. His ability to come up with random fake facts that often spun into full stories disguised as fact and documentary was a personality trait that both made her laugh and roll her eyes. Today, Ana's laugh only thinly veiled her sadness in watching her husband slowly fade away from who he had been before the disease. From the day they received his terminal diagnosis, Ana struggled to remain strong for John. For his part, John continued to keep a lighthearted attitude to life, despite fearing the inevitable result of his diagnosis.

To their friends, Ana was known as the strong one in the relationship, while John was the happy-go-lucky jovial person. But John's bright take on life was more often than not a disguise for the strength he had for his wife when she needed it. Ana was, as John often described her, a puff pastry, because she seemed hard on the outside but was filled with a soft gooey sweetness that everyone loved. And in truth he was right: the hard exterior which Ana showed to the world was easily cracked, leaving her exposed. This is where she would rely on what she always saw as John's hidden strength.

"Annie, did you know that during the Tang Dynasty, the Emperor's cooks deliberately under-spiced his food when he fell ill? And as a result, Emperor Gaozong ruled for thirty-two years! On his death tablet he had it inscribed that his longevity was due to horribly bland food prepared by his most honoured cooks." John smiled as he elaborated on his story.

Ana smiled while holding back tears. "John, how on earth are you still so full of shit?"

"Huh? No, no, babe, these are incontrovenible facts."

"Incontrovertible," Ana responded.

"What?"

"You mean 'incontrovertible' facts can't be disputed. Incontrovenible isn't a word."

"Exactly! You agree they are incontrovertible facts." John held his spoon in his mouth while looking at Ana with a mischievous smile. All she could do was roll her eyes at him and they laughed at each other.

John's laughter was interrupted by a coughing fit. Initially he continued to laugh through the coughs, but eventually he was unable to continue as the cough caused him to gasp for air. As he caught his breath, both were reminded of their reality, temporarily forgotten thanks to his foolish storytelling.

After a momentary silence, Ana wiped tears from her eyes and asked, "How am I supposed to continue without you, John? I don't know if I can do this without you."

Putting his hand on hers, he looked into his wife's eyes with a serious look. "Ana, you've never been alone since the day we met, and I promise you that you'll never be alone. I will always be with you." John held Ana's hand silently and let the gravity of the situation settle for both of them. Neither of them spoke for the next few hours. Ana lay beside her husband as they watched TV. Somehow, despite his frail state, Ana felt a sense of security and protection lying beside John, his arm around her. She couldn't lie *on* him, as even the weight of her head on his chest caused him pain and made it difficult for him to breath.

"Annie, you should probably head home," John whispered into her ear.

"I'm okay, John. I'll spend the night here."

"No, you never sleep when you're here, and you're a mess the next day. I'll see you tomorrow after work. I'm going to be sleeping most of the day, anyway. We'll both sleep better this way."

"I know, but I hate leaving you here."

"I'm fine, Annie."

Ana sat up and kissed John on the forehead. "Please don't give the nurses a hard time with your foolish stories tomorrow, John," she said with a smile. This time the sadness in her eyes was replaced with an adoration and love that she had for John's playful nature.

"Never, Annie. Only incontrovertible facts."

"Good. I'll see you tomorrow."

"Tomorrow."

At five the following morning Ana received a call from St. Joseph's hospital. John had died in his sleep. The nurse said that he died peacefully, comfortably and not in pain. But despite this, Ana felt that she had abandoned John to face his final moments alone. He may have left this world without pain, but because she left him in the hospital alone on his final night she suffered beyond anything she could have imagined.

The night of John's funeral, Ana sat in their home looking through his belongings. Over the years, John had amassed an eclectic collection of books, trinkets and memorabilia. Ana had often left him to his "office," which was little more than a spare room full of books with an old desk that, despite its weathered and deteriorating appearance, managed to stand. She had asked him numerous times to get a new desk; she even offered to have it brought to the house. Time after time, he'd respond the same way: "And get rid of this old beaut? Annie, this desk is a classic; it holds so many great secrets." His romanticism for old things was infectious, and she'd relent every time he boasted about the features of the desk, or any of his weird and wonderful things. Ana sat in the room looking at the mix of books, figurines and coins, and cried. Before, she couldn't understand why he held on to readings from second-year university, or an antique typewriter or such, with more conviction than he had for his degree or accolades from work. Looking around now, she realized that this room represented John's soul more than anything else in their home. She could imagine him in the room with her, emphatically trying his best to explain how each item held the same level of importance as the last. His hands would be waving in the air wildly and darting around as he his face glowed with enthusiasm for each and every reason he gave her.

Ana's thoughts were broken by the doorbell. She hadn't been paying attention to the time and the whole night had passed sitting in John's office. Quickly, she jumped up and ran to the door to see who was calling.

She had forgotten that her sister Danica was coming over. Yesterday, Danica had wanted to spend the night, but she didn't want anyone around. She wanted the chance to be alone in the house to take a moment by herself. "I'm not going to have anyone babysit me. If I can't spend the night alone, I will find a way to get used to it," Ana had said to Danica after the funeral. Her strong personality often led her to wanting to go it alone. This was often tempered and contrasted by John's more social approach to things. The day of his funeral, as was often the case in their relationship, she put her best foot forward and showed that she didn't need people's help. Ana would even joke that if not for John they probably wouldn't have any friends, to which John would sarcastically respond, "No, Ana, you'd just build us one." Now with Danica arriving, Ana's first concern was that her sister would see that she'd been up all night. She quickly tried to straighten her hair and make herself look more put together than she was and went to open the door.

"Hey," Ana said, opening the door.

"Hey, hon, how are you?" Danica asked.

"As good as I can be, really."

"Did you sleep?"

"Uh, yeah a bit."

"You look like you've been up all night. Did you sleep in your clothes from yesterday?" Danica asked, touching Ana's arm.

Gently pulling away, Ana said sheepishly, "Yeah, I kinda let time get away from me last night. I thought I was fine, but I started going through some of John's stuff in his office and just got lost thinking about things." Taking a breath to help hold back tears, Ana continued, "I don't know if I can imagine life without him, Dee. I always knew that I loved him, but I didn't realize that his quirkiness was such a huge part of my life. I was sitting in his office, surrounded by all his stuff, and I could see how the fact that none of it belonged together made it more and more indicative of his personality."

"Ana, it's normal to feel lost and sad. You don't have to do this by yourself."

"I know, Dee, but it's just so hard. When I got to a point that I couldn't do things by myself, I would have John, and I relied on him so much. I never let anyone, even him, know how important he was to me. Now I'm alone without him."

"You don't have to be alone, Ana. You have people around that want to and will help you if you need anything."

They finally sat down in Ana's kitchen and Danica began preparing coffee. Danica began shuffling through the various coffee mugs before picking one up and looking at her sister.

"Why do you guys have so many small coffee mugs?"

"That's John. He always said, 'If you need a big coffee, it isn't much of a coffee, now is it?'" They looked at each other in silence for a moment before breaking into laughter. Ana dropped her head to the countertop with her hands out. "Dee, this is exactly what I mean! He's even in the coffee cups." Ana's laughter gradually turned to crying and Danica ran over to her sister, putting her arms around her.

"Ana, it's okay."

"No, Dee, it isn't. Everything is changed and now I have to find a way in this new reality. It's all fucked up now. I love him so much, and everything in this house reminds me of him. It's all him and me and I can't separate that."

Hugging her sister harder, she said, "I know, Ana, and I'll do everything I can to help you through this. I will be here for you, and I know it won't be the same as having John here, but I'll do whatever I can to make it easier for you."

"Thank you."

As days turned to weeks and weeks to months, Ana slowly began to accept her new reality. Danica stayed with her for the first few weeks after the funeral, but even that had to come to an end, as the constant travel to and from work and being away from her children began to take a toll on Danica. But with time, Ana became accustomed to being alone, and realized she would be able to live in her home without John. Eventually, Ana spent less time in John's office, although she wouldn't change anything about it. His books and trinkets remained exactly where they were the day he left home for the last time. She didn't avoid the office, but slowly, as her emotional wounds healed, she found she had less reason to be in there. Month after month, Ana would only go into the office to clean it, which seemed to be less necessary as she spent less time in the house. She was moving on with her life, able to recover and become the person she was before.

A year after John's death, as Ana was cleaning the office, she sat in John's chair, looking around at his belongings. "What am I supposed to do with all of this?" she said to herself. "I don't want to get rid of it, but how am I supposed to keep these things that remind me of you and still find a way to move forward with my life?" She picked up a book that had been sitting on the desk for the last year and thumbed through the pages. "John, I didn't even know you had an interest in Korean history. Although, to be fair, you probably didn't know that you had an interest in it before you bought the book, either."

She noticed a small white moth sitting on one of the bookshelves, slowly moving its wings. She watched with a small bit of curiosity, wondering where it came from as she didn't have the window open in the room. The moth began to fly, and it fluttered around the room, almost jumping up and down in the air, like it was spelling out the notes on a staff. The moth fluttered from left to right across the room before landing on an old globe that John kept on a plant stand in the office. Ana stood and walked out from behind the desk to where the moth remained perched on top of the globe to get a closer look. As she approached it, she tried to lean slowly in to get a closer look. The moth's appearance fascinated Ana: all white with what appeared to be a mane of fine hairs around the back of its head. Behind this were two small white antennae poking up in the air. Its all-white wings seemed to be edged with the same white hair, giving it an elegant appearance. The moth seemed to stare back at her, its two small antennae twitching above its black eyes. All of a sudden, the moth flew from its spot on top of the world and fluttered up into Ana's face, causing her to shut her eyes and pull back. When she opened her eyes, the moth was fluttering around the room above the desk where she had been sitting.

"You little shit, you almost flew into my eyes!"

The moth bounced around the air as it had before, but it was now flying from above the desk toward Ana, standing by the globe, then fluttering back to the desk.

"Well, obviously I scared you."

The moth settled into its flight pattern and circled above the desk before landing on a lamp near the corner of the desk. It was again facing Ana, its little antennae twitching and wings flapping slowly as it had before it flew into Ana's face.

"Now you're just trying to mock me, aren't you?" Ana said, smiling.

She slowly walked over to the moth again to watch it as it sat perched on the lamp. The antennae stopped moving momentarily and Ana stopped walking.

"Come on now, you're in my house, you can't go and get scared because I'm coming to get a closer look at you."

The moth began twitching its antennae again and Ana smiled at it. Before she could get any closer, the moth jumped from its perch again and began flying around the room. Ana stood straight up and watched as the little white moth fluttered in circles near the ceiling of the room. Ana smiled with her hands on her hips and laughed to herself.

"You're just playing a game now, aren't you? Every time I get close you seem to jump up and fly around just to get me to move to another place."

Seemingly still writing sheet music in the air, the little white moth fluttered down to another place in the room, now landing on the first bookshelf that Ana had noticed it on. This time the moth landed facing away from Ana, who remained standing still. She thought she could slowly sneak up on the moth to get a closer look at it. Ever so lightly, Ana took little steps toward the bookshelf where the little white moth sat facing the books that John had long ago placed in an order he best understood.

"That's good, little guy, you just try and figure out what John was thinking when he put those books there and I'll come over and take a look at you," Ana said as she cartoonishly tiptoed toward the moth.

Just as she got close enough to get a look at the moth, it again took flight and fluttered up into the air near the ceiling of the room.

"Oh, you little shit! You just won't let me get close to you, will you. Why did you even come in here?"

Ana decided she was giving up on getting a close look at the moth and sat back in the chair. She leaned back, crossed her legs and watched as the little moth flew around the room, landed, and then flew again. It continued to circle in the air near the ceiling before erratically bouncing down to where Ana was seated behind the desk.

The moth fluttered down to Ana and right into her face. Instinctively, Ana reeled back, swatted at it, and struck it with her right hand, knocking it out of the air.

"Oh no! Why did you do that?" Ana jumped out of her chair and looked at the moth on the floor. "Jesus, what were you thinking?"

The moth twitched and jumped about the floor turning in chaotic circles. One wing was clearly injured and prevented the little creature from being able to fly. In a panicked attempt at survival, the moth jumped and spun circle after circle before it came to a rest on an envelope that was shyly peeking out from beneath one of John's bookshelves. Looking down at the creature, Ana's heart seemed to sink in her chest as its movements became slower and more laboured. The one wing that could still move struggled against its fate as slowly it opened and painfully it returned. The antennae, after a moment, seemed to calm in their movements and the moth appeared to contentedly accept its fate.

Sitting back on its hindmost legs, the little white moth seemed to look up at Ana in its final moments with a sense of comfort and acceptance. Ana couldn't explain why she felt the moth seemed to look at her this way, but in her mind and in her heart she knew it wasn't fearful of anything in this moment and was content to have been in the room with her. Or perhaps she was content to have been in the room with the moth.

The darkness gradually faded and was replaced with small streams of light. The dim light slowly brightened and the pain in John's head diminished. With a stretch and a groan, he found himself lying on his back in a light-soaked field. Sitting up, he looked around and took in the view of a field in bloom. The depth of green from the grass was beautifully contrasted by the rainbow of colours from the seemingly infinite number of flowers. It all reminded him of a bright, warm, spring morning. It all caused him to break down.

Sobbing into his hands, John thought about his wife, about the chance he just had to see her. As the little white moth, he did all he could to be with her again and be close to her. Yet all his effort was for nothing. Ana didn't know it was him; it was something that she could never have known. Seared into his mind were her bright blue eyes and chocolate-brown hair. All he wanted to do was to see her one more time. Foolishly, John thought that if he could bring himself to Ana he would be able to take both her pain and his away, yet all he did was amplify the agony he felt.

He was left with the realization that the time he had to help Ana was gone, and only the passing of time could do anything to help her heal. The further time moved forward, the deeper his sorrow grew, and it wasn't her healing that was at question anymore, it was his pain and sorrow from having to exist in an eternity where he could not be beside Ana, which continued to torture him through every passing moment.

"What kind of existence is this that I have to choose between never seeing my wife again or returning to her in the form of a moth?" John cried as he sobbed in his hands. He knew he had to get a hold of his emotions and control himself; nothing else would allow him to survive in this afterlife without losing what was left of his mind.

What seemed like days and weeks passed, and through nearly every moment John contemplated what he should do. "Do I try to go back to her again? There is no way she will know that I am the moth. But I'd die a thousand deaths to be with her again for another fleeting moment," John said to himself as he walked around the blooming meadow. He had contemplated his eternity and wondered if he could stand to see his wife another time, to lose her again and have to return to the meadow once more. Nothing stopped him from returning other than his fear of the inevitable repeated loss. He knew Ana would never know it was him returning, and she would, like time, move on and her life would not stop despite his absence.

John was again temporarily blinded by the intensity of the light replacing darkness. His eyes slowly adjusted, and by the time he was able to see again he began to feel his wings. Looking back was no longer an option, but he could he tell they were there again. Slowly he opened them and returned them to their natural resting position. Open, pause, close, pause. The world around him, so familiar, now seemed oddly foreign.

Flying in through an open window, John realized the house was changed. The colour of the walls was no longer his; the furniture which adorned each room was not that which he and Ana had picked to decorate their home. This place, although the same building, was not the home he had lived in and remembered. Life had moved on without him, and everything that was once familiar was no longer present in the home. It was a house that he knew his way around, but no longer the home he had left.

Fluttering to the second level of the house, John heard a female voice, one that was unlike any he was familiar with. It was nothing like Ana's—this was the voice of a child. To the voice he flew until he found her in his office. But it was his office no more. The walls were not covered in bookshelves lined with books and trinkets collected over a life of work and exploration. They were colourfully painted yet bare and, to his eye, cold.

Landing on a lamp sitting on a table beside a soft chair in the corner, his anonymous exploration of the house that was once his home ended. The little girl behind the voice took notice of the little white moth perched on a lamp in the room where she now played and he once read. Her eyes filled with wonder and curiosity, her face painted with childhood joy. Immediately, she dropped the toys she was playing with and rose to her feet. The young girl watched as the little white moth and its little white antennae moved back and forth. She giggled with wonder at this pretty little moth as its wings opened and paused, closed and paused.

Unsure of what to feel, John stared at the little girl. This was not why he had returned to this house. His love for which he had wished to die a thousand deaths was long removed from this place. Ana's life was uncertain, her afterlife unknown. The emptiness he felt was a chasm that filled his soul. Yet the childish joy in the little girl's face that stared at him now seemed to take his attention and steal away from the thoughts of despair that lingered in and around his mind. Life had moved on, and he wandered the world seeking what was once there but had long since passed. In moving on, the world he returned to had manifested a new happiness which, in his state, he could never had imagined. John sat pondering his existence, and he slowly opened his wings, paused, and closed them again.

Lost in his conflicting thoughts of despair and hope, John failed to see the plastic cup in the hands of the little girl. She covered him where he stood and laughed with excitement.

The little white moth jumped and bounced within the cup, captivating her attention. She knew where it came from, but it was such a joy to have this little pretty white moth with her in her room. She told the moth everything she was doing. "This is for tea. Do you drink tea?" she asked the little white moth. With each question, its wings opened and closed and it jumped and danced. Each dance and movement made her smile, and with each dance and movement she paid it more attention than the moment before.

John couldn't help but be captivated by the happiness in the little girl's face, the joy in her laughter at his every movement. This was nothing that he had planned for in returning to the house; he hadn't planned to see this little girl or to be the focus of her childlike attention. All he had desired was to return to see the woman he loved, but she had long since left this place. Not since the night in the hospital had John been the focus of such attention, of such innocent love. But the little girl left the room in which she had captured him in the plastic cup. He wondered when she would return to be captivated by the dancing little moth once more. But as days turned to nights and nights turned to days, the little white moth was left where it was, under the little plastic cup in the little room that was once a study, alone and forgotten, and ready to return to the meadow where he would not sleep, nor would he see his Ana anymore.